HIDE AND SEEK

Also by Rachel Kramer Bussel
He's on Top
She's on Top
Crossdressing
Best Sex Writing 2008
Caught Looking (with Alison Tyler)

Also by Alison Tyler
Best Bondage Erotica
Best Bondage Erotica 2
Exposed
The Happy Birthday Book of Erotica
Heat Wave: Sizzling Sex Stories
Luscious: Stories of Anal Eroticism
The Merry XXXmas Book of Erotica
Red Hot Erotica
Slave to Love
Three-Way
Caught Looking (with Rachel Kramer Bussel)
A Is for Amour
B Is for Bondage
C Is for Coeds
D Is for Dress-Up
E Is for Exotic
F Is for Fetish
G Is for Games
H Is for Hardcore
Got a Minute?
Love at First Sting

HIDE AND SEEK
21 TALES OF EXHIBITIONISM & VOYEURISM

Edited by
Rachel Kramer Bussel
and Alison Tyler

Copyright © 2007 by Rachel Kramer Bussel and Alison Tyler.

All rights reserved. Except for brief passages quoted in newspaper, magazine, radio, or television reviews, no part of this book may be reproduced in any form or by any means, electronic or mechanical, including photocopying or recording, or by information storage or retrieval system, without permission in writing from the publisher.

Published in the United States by Cleis Press Inc.,
P.O. Box 14697, San Francisco, California 94114.

Printed in the United States.
Cover design: Scott Idleman
Cover photo: Getty Images
Text design: Frank Wiedemann
Cleis Press logo art: Juana Alicia
First Edition.
10 9 8 7 6 5 4 3 2 1

They flee from me that sometime did me seek
With naked foot, stalking in my chamber.
—Sir Thomas Wyatt

Golly jeepers
Where'd you get those peepers?
Peepshow, creepshow
Where did you get those eyes?
—Siouxsie & the Banshees

Contents

- ix   *Introduction: Watch and Learn* • ALISON TYLER
- xiii   *Introduction: Showing Off in Style* • RACHEL KRAMER BUSSEL

- 1   *Counting the Days* • SASKIA WALKER
- 13   *Red Light, Green Light* • SHANNA GERMAIN
- 22   *The Corners of My Eyes* • STAN KENT
- 34   *Interview with a Porn Star* • RADCLYFFE
- 42   *Operator 84* • THOMAS S. ROCHE
- 47   *Glint* • PORTIA DA COSTA
- 54   *The Craziest Thing* • GWEN MASTERS
- 64   *For All the World to See* • MATT CONKLIN
- 76   *The Astronomer* • L.A. MISTRAL
- 86   *Visual Memory* • TERESA NOELLE ROBERTS
- 94   *A Girl, Two Guys, and a Sex Toy* • KRISTINA WRIGHT
- 102   *Operatic Ecstasy* • ERICA DEQUAYA
- 112   *Behind the Wheel* • L. ELISE BLAND
- 119   *She Grinds Her Own Coffee* • CHERI MAGID
- 130   *Peeping Tom, Dick, and Harriet* • MICHELLE HOUSTON
- 137   *Undoing the Laces* • ANDREA DALE
- 144   *Cruising* • LEE CAIRNEY
- 150   *Roof Flashing* • DEBRA HYDE
- 158   *Watching* • DANTE DAVIDSON
- 163   *Not a Voyeur* • ALISON TYLER
- 170   *Like This* • RACHEL KRAMER BUSSEL

- 179   About the Authors
- 185   About the Editors

INTRODUCTION: WATCH AND LEARN

Oh, yeah, I like to watch almost as much as I like to be watched. Almost.
—Radclyffe

I am always watching. Memorizing. Capturing. I pay attention to everyone around me, growing silent sometimes in crowds so that I can be sure I haven't missed something important.

I eavesdrop.

I spy.

Can't help myself. So I don't even bother to try. And that's what made reading the stories for *Hide and Seek* so fucking hot. I was eavesdropping once more, able to view the fantasies—my favorite types of fantasies—right up close. What I especially like about the voyeur/exhibitionist fetish are the two halves of the puzzle. The way they fit so neatly together. The stories in this book fit just as well…

Do you want to watch your woman pick up a hot guy to fuck?

Lizzie and Next Big Thing danced; they danced closer, bodies brushing. They kissed, and they retired to the bar. They shared cocktails. They felt each other out with conversation. They kissed some more. His hand slipped to her ass. At some point he asked for her number. She told him she had a boyfriend, but she was allowed to play around as long as he could watch. ("The Corners of My Eyes")

Or do you want to get busy in the cab ride home, while the sultry female taxi driver watches in her rearview mirror?

I can tell you're going to come, and now we're clear of the midtown traffic, hurtling down Eighth Avenue at a breakneck pace. It's almost like the cab driver is in competition with us, trying to see if she can get us where we're going before we can finish. ("Operator 84")

Would you like to fuck on the beach while strangers watch you with binoculars?

I ought to be outraged at the thought of somebody spying on me while Gavin and I are making love, but the idea's got into my head now, and I've a feeling it's stuck there. Instead of tilting the parasol so that our distant watcher—or watchers—can't see us, I get up, take hold of it, and twist it around out of the way so it doesn't obstruct their view. And while I'm up here, I lift my arms and do a sort of supermodel thing, pushing my hair back from my face in a way that makes my boobs rise in my bikini top and salute the sun. ("Glint")

Or do you desire being the one peering out a window?

She bent her head back and cupped his cock in her hands and tipped it up. Then she opened her mouth.

Thomas breathed in short, hungry bursts. His whole body pressed into the telescope, rocking it with the rhythms he was seeing. ("The Astronomer")

INTRODUCTION: WATCH AND LEARN

You can be on display for a crowd full of anonymous, hungry watchers:

All around the room were windows—ten in all, with black slats covering them. Soon, a person would be behind each window. Customers who had paid would watch the slats go up and see into the room where we were standing. This was so they could watch us make love. There was no way for us to see into the rooms. Each window was a two-way mirror. They could see in, but we couldn't see out. It would give the illusion of privacy. ("Peeping Tom, Dick, and Harriet")

Or is it enough to simply *think* people know what you're doing, to wonder if they know?

She was standing before she knew she had done it. She should take her purse. Should she take her purse?... She took out her wallet. She put it back. She picked up her whole bag again. Was Silvio watching? Was his daughter? ("She Grinds Her Own Coffee")

Better yet, why choose? Hide with the characters in half the stories, seek with those naughty players in the other. Get turned on by them all.

At least, that's what *I* did.

XXX,
Alison Tyler

INTRODUCTION: SHOWING OFF IN STYLE

Compared to all the other sexual acts one could engage in, voyeurism and exhibitionism may seem a bit passive. Watching, spying, ogling. Teasing, flaunting, putting oneself on display. But the characters in *Hide and Seek* push the envelope by finding new and inventive ways to spy and be spied on, letting us know just how active, enthusiastic, and passionate they have to be to get what they want the most.

From windows to rooftops to webcams, these naughty boys and girls take pleasure wherever they can find it. That might be in the backseat of a cab, knowing the driver's clocking every move, or putting on a live vibrator sex show for one's husband. They might be going about their workday, only to find that a stranger has a little show-and-tell of the adult variety in mind.

I tend to think that all writers are exhibitionists of some sort, begging readers to feast their eyes on our most salacious output. We want people to watch us get naked as we explore our deepest fantasies, the kinds that make us blush and squirm and shift in our seats. We want to offer up a piece of ourselves to you, letting you look to your heart's content. But we writers are also voyeurs, constantly absorbing everything around us, our eyes zooming in on the pertinent details, the little moments that make sex all the hotter for their simplicity. We notice the details, and we want you to know that we're watching your every move. Don't think that sigh or ankle crossing or primping or cleavage or erection has gone unnoticed; we're watching and we like what we see.

In many of these stories, characters are made to wait, wish, and fantasize. There's no telling just when your favoring Peeping Tom will return to rake his eyes all over your body and make you feel naked even when you're not. There's no telling when she'll bring home a plaything and offer him to you for the price of a sex show. There's no telling when you'll find yourself in public, in flagrante, being seen—and savored. The opportunities for quality viewing or flaunting of the sexual sort can't be called up as easily as pay-per-view. You have to strike while the iron is hot, or keep your eyes peeled for the hottie who can't wait to strip down just for you. It's this search for the perfect partner to complement their kink that makes so many of these stories soar. Without an accomplice, they're just putting on a solo performance, but having a pair (or more) of eyes trained on you while you get off can bring out the inner porn star in all of us.

So instead of passivity, maybe what the successful voyeur and exhibitionist need is cunning, timing, talent. Yes, it's a skill you can be good at, knowing when to push your lover to give you more and when to back off. Knowing when it's okay to forget about the opera on stage and create your own right there in your seat. Knowing when that blow job she's about to give you is just too picture-perfect not to capture on film. Knowing when to stay put and pass on a threesome in favor of seeing her writhing in the arms of another man. All these tricks of the trade

INTRODUCTION: SHOWING OFF IN STYLE

and more are revealed in this steamy collection of stories where anything can happen.

And if you want to test your own talent for showing off, don't just hide this book at home tucked away under the covers. Go ahead, I dare you, and read it at the park, on the subway, on an airplane. Read it where you know people will be watching. Or read it in a corner of a busy room where you can raise your head between stories and train your eyes on the person you most desire. Maybe you'll discover you're a natural.

Rachel Kramer Bussel

COUNTING THE DAYS

Saskia Walker

Thank God it's Friday. I'd been counting the days off—and, boy, had they ever dragged. But I figured that if I could get to the end of the first week, I could maybe make it into week two. Maybe.

I just had to prove I could last through my one-month contract. Biting the bullet and taking an office job had been the absolute pits in the first place, but I couldn't drift from college course to college course any longer. The time had come to quell my rebellious streak, tame my multicolored mop, take out my nose ring, and don an acceptably smart outfit. *What a crime*, I thought to myself, when I'd packed away my usual, much more alternative wardrobe and headed for the temp agency.

The job I was assigned to was deadly. I was audio-typing debt-collection letters for a junior lawyer, and William had been junior forever. He stumbled into my office, blushing to the roots of his remaining few hairs, and deposited a stack of files and tapes on my desk. That was day one. Since day two, he'd left the stacks on my desk before I even got in, presumably in order not to have to make small talk with me, and then disappeared off to who knew where. Maybe he was expecting a simpering office mouse, not a frustrated rebel who responded sarcastically when he mentioned the pleasant weather we were having for the time of year.

Well, what did he expect?

The weather was outside the tinted windows and I was trapped inside. There was no decent company to chat with on breaks, and there wasn't even any eye candy in the vicinity. The building site opposite my nineteenth-story window was too far away to make out anything. That would have been something. All I got was a drifting tide of muck curtaining my window courtesy of the builder's activities—no brawny guys to check out. Perhaps if I brought in a pair of binoculars I could get a better look, and if I got a better look, that might break up the monotony.

Mostly there was just me and Audrey in the offices. Audrey was the senior administrator, and she sat reading magazines and filing her nails all day in the reception. She looked down her nose at me condescendingly whenever I came out of my cell for a coffee. The highlight of her work schedule seemed to be shuffling wannabe-divorcées into the senior partner's office, giving appropriate murmurs of concern to their irate monologues about truant husbands. I wouldn't have been able to keep a straight face. Perhaps that's why I wasn't on the front desk.

Looking at the clock, I stood up. It was nearly midday, time for my third caffeine shot of the day. I was about to step out from behind my desk when darkness descended and I froze. A shadow had fallen across me from behind, from the window situated behind my desk. The shadow moved across the surface of the desk. My heart beat faster as I tried to make sense of it.

Nothing had broken the light falling in the window all week. What could it be?

I turned and took in the sight that met my eyes. Standing in a suspended safety cradle was a window cleaner moving a large squeegee over the surface of the glass with a rhythmic agility, all the while watching me and grinning cheekily. He winked, obviously well aware he'd given me a fright. I managed to return his smile and wave at him, snatching up my cup from the desk to cover my awkwardness.

Something interesting had finally happened! And, *yes*, he was interesting. Ruggedly good-looking, with several days' worth of stubble—tall, well-built, and bleached blond. He went about his work in a showy, nonchalant way that made it look like a warm-up for dirty dancing. He moved his entire body as if dancing to the music he was listening to on his headset, and rode his massive squeegee easily over the surface of the glass, his biceps flexing, his torso riding firm and strong beneath the T-shirt he was wearing. Sexy! My blood pumped quicker when I noticed he was eyeing me speculatively, from head to toe. I leaned one hip up against the desk, toying with the mug in my hands, eyeing up the sight. Well, why not? He was doing the same.

When he finished his task, he dropped the squeegee and reached into his pocket and pulled something out. He scribbled on the piece of paper with a stub of pencil, then held it up against the glass for me to read. I stepped closer and read the scrawled message:

GREAT LEGS. NEXT TIME WEAR A SHORTER SKIRT.

I smiled, I couldn't help it. He grinned, saluted, and hit a control panel, hanging easily on the ropes as the safety cradle disappeared from view.

Well, that had woken me up. Wear a shorter skirt? What a cad! Sure, I was up for some fun and games, especially with a hunk like him, but when was the "next time" that he was referring to? There was only one way to find out.

"I just had the most amazing shock," I said to Audrey as I poured filter coffee into my mug. "Some guy was hanging on the outside of the building cleaning the windows."

Audrey gave me a superior smile. "Not what you expect to see this high up, is it?"

"Not exactly. How often do they come around? I'd like to be prepared next time."

"Oh, usually every six weeks."

My heart sank. I'd be finished with my contract and gone by the next time he appeared.

"Until they started the building work opposite," she added. "It's every Friday on that side of the building now, so you'll have to be prepared for another visit next week."

"Oh, I will be." I sidled off, trying to contain my smile.

That second week went much quicker. In fact, counting the days till Friday took on a whole new meaning. I was looking forward to my visitor, instead of wishing the days away until the end of my contract. I didn't even think of bringing the binoculars in; I had something far more interesting to focus on: the arrival of the dishy window cleaner. What would happen if I did as he suggested and wore a shorter skirt? Where would it go then? I raced through my stacks of audio-typing while at the back of my mind I tried to decide what to wear.

Audrey commented on the fact that my typing had speeded up. She had so little to do, she had to eavesdrop on me to fill her timetable. If it wasn't for the prospect of the window guy, I would have told her to stick her job. She didn't approve of me, that much was obvious from the start. I'd heard her on the phone to the temp agency, asking if they had "anyone more suitable, someone the right caliber to work in a legal office."

Too bad for her they didn't have anyone else, right? And she *so* did not approve when I arrived for work on that second Friday, wearing the leather miniskirt I usually saved for clubbing, knee-length boots, and a skin-tight, lizard-print shirt that dipped low into my cleavage. I waved when I passed her desk, where she sat open-mouthed, glaring at my outfit.

The morning went far too slowly, and I was up and pacing around between the desk and the window when the shadow of the cradle finally began to descend. And this time I was even more mesmerized, because as the window cleaner lowered into my field of vision I realized he was stripped to the waist. Boy, what a sight for sore eyes that was. He was built, all right, all that physical work had given him a great body, and the day was warm enough for him to sun himself while he worked. He grinned, eyeing me appreciatively as he washed the window. I reached for a piece of paper and wrote him a message:

GREAT ABS! DO YOU APPROVE OF THE SKIRT LENGTH?

When he broke into a laugh, I'd have paid dearly to hear the sound of it. He nodded, his mouth forming a whistle while he eyed the gap between my boots and the skirt. With his eyes on me like that, I was suddenly aware of every inch of my body. My breasts felt tight. My sex was heavy, responsive to every signal he was giving me, to every nuance in his body language. I turned on my heel and gave him a better look, hands on hips. He reached into his pocket and scribbled on his notepad, slamming the paper against the glass:

OH YEAH, THAT'S MUCH BETTER.
BUT I STILL CAN'T SEE WHAT COLOR YOUR UNDERWEAR IS.

I laughed. What a lad. And something about the setup, with him on the other side of the glass like that, made me feel even more daring than I might have been under normal circumstances. I was no shrinking violet, either way.

His squeegee was hanging idly in one hand; the other leaned up against the taut ropes of the safety cradle as he watched, riveted, while I slid one finger down into the front of my shirt, idly toying with the top button in my cleavage. He licked his lips. My sex clenched; my panties were already damp with expectation. Seeing him through the barrier of the impermeable glass had created a void of discovery, a safe zone to test each other out. I popped my top button, thrilled by the effect I was having on him. He mouthed something encouraging. I let another button pop open. He nodded, one hand gesturing for me to continue. I felt like I was part of an act in a live sex show. The thought spurred me on. I stepped closer to the glass. We were possibly twelve inches apart, but he was so untouchable. I undid the final two buttons, my hands pushing the fabric back to reveal my sheer lace bra.

He shook his head, his eyes glazed, and ran one finger down the length of the glass in front of my breasts, smearing the damp glass with his touch. He continued to stare while he grappled in his pocket for his paper and pencil and wrote me another note:

WILL I GET TO SEE MORE OF YOU NEXT WEEK?

He scrunched the paper in his hand after I read it, and his eyes were molten with arousal. I nodded and blew him a kiss, winking. As he reached for the controls on his cradle, his other hand ran over the impressive bulge in his jeans, and he flickered his eyebrows at me. Then he was gone. Only the smear on the glass remained to remind me of what had passed between us, a sticky remark on the intervening sheer pane. I touched the inside of the glass, placing my own mark against his. Man, was he ever sexy. And he was making me so hot. I stalked over to the air-conditioning panel and turned it up to full blast, my mind racing with ideas of how to up the ante the following week.

By the time that third Friday came around, I'd been thinking on it long and hard, to the extent that I'd even dreamed about the guy twice. Both times it was the live sex show imagery, and the idea fascinated me. In the first dream, I was dancing for him, slow and sexy. He was riveted, sitting back in a low chair, his erection straining through his jeans. In the second dream, I stripped naked and then watched as he tried to lick my body through the glass. When I woke, I was twisted in my sheets, my fingers crushed between my legs as I wanked myself off.

My excitement levels built over the week, and my imagination was running riot. To top it all, Audrey had pissed me off big time, which left me feeling even more rebellious. I was ready to pull pints in my local pub rather than listen to her miserable condescension a moment longer. That sense of rebellion and the fact the guy had filled my thoughts all week long meant that I was edgy with rebellion and high on my own physical arousal.

Thank God it's Friday, I murmured to myself, yet again. But this time I smiled at the idea.

The window cleaner looked at my floating summer dress with a surprised expression when he winched down into view. I waved and then turned my chair to face the window, to face him. I sat down in it, staring straight at him, smiling. He wrote his message:

HEY, YOU'RE BREAKING MY HEART HERE.
THAT SKIRT IS WAY TOO LONG.

He mimed an aching heart, his expression teasing me all the while. I shook my head at him, swinging my chair from side to side, then I kicked back in the chair, one strappy, sandaled foot jamming up against the window frame, the dress sliding down my thighs and pooling in my groin.

Oh, yeah, he loved that.

I pivoted on one heel, my chair moving from side to side. I knew he was watching the flash of scarlet G-string I was wearing, and it fueled my fire. Between my thighs, a nagging pulse begged for attention. I let my hand tease along the hemline of the dress. He lifted his head, his eyes on my fingers. I picked up the piece of paper I'd left handy and scribbled on it:

WHAT DO YOU THINK NOW?

Quickly, he replied:

I'D LIKE TO PUT MY HANDS UNDER IT AND TOUCH YOU.

It was just the kind of response that I'd hoped for. He was really up for this. I ran my hand over the surface of my G-string, one finger sliding beneath the fabric. He nodded his head, scribbling again:

YOU ARE SO BAD!

"You better believe it," I whispered, as I pushed my fingers into my damp slit, where my clit was begging for attention. With a quick, practiced action, I arrested it between two fingers, my whole body jolting with the sensations that instantaneously roared over me.

The guy started craning his neck, as if he could see inside my underwear if he tried hard enough. Logic had clearly gone from his mind by that point. For me, the fact that one gorgeous man was watching, wanting me, completely mesmerized by what I was doing, was like a drug heightening the experience, channeling every dart of pleasure into a major roller-coaster ride. I slid down in the chair, my back arching against it as I worked my clit. My fingers were sticky, the flimsy fabric of my G-string quickly growing wet. His mouth was moving; he was saying something to himself, and his eyes were glazed with lust.

"Yes," I whispered at his silent form. "Yes." I managed to nod at him, my lips parting, when my clit throbbed unbearably and density gathered in my core. As I rode the wave, I became aware that he was moving. The cradle was disappearing out of view. Had I gone too far? Had I embarrassed the poor guy? I doubted it—he'd pushed it along this far. And I'd really got off on the secret, silent performance for the man on the other side of the glass. My body was thrumming with sensation, my energy levels soaring.

I let my foot slide down from the window. I couldn't help thinking about how it might have looked to him, from the outside. Perhaps he'd gone off somewhere more discreet to have a wank. The idea infused me with a sense of raw power, heady and intoxicating. That was when I heard voices outside.

"Fuck." I tried to pull myself together.

There was some sort of disagreement going on in the corridor. Audrey sounded put out. I grappled my dress into place, spinning my chair to face front. The door sprang open.

"There must be some mistake," Audrey said, in a bewildered tone. "We had the interiors done just a few weeks ago."

"It's contracted, trust me."

I blinked, several times. It was him. He was there, standing in the doorway to my office. He'd put his T-shirt on, come inside, and found my office—and now he was walking inside. Dumping a bucket on the floor, he grinned at me and slammed the door shut behind him. A stifled cry of dismay emitted from the hallway.

Now what was I going to do? No glass shield, no gap the equivalent of thousands of square feet separating us. My blood roared, my heart thumping out a fierce rhythm. Given that I was already totally wired by what had gone before, his 100 percent physical presence tripped switches I didn't even know I had.

"Sorry to interrupt, but I couldn't resist." He put his hands on his hips, observing me with hungry, watchful eyes. He was even sexier in the flesh, or so it seemed, and the sound of his voice ran torrents of sensation over me. I was delirious with arousal, unable to stop myself responding in kind.

"Couldn't resist seeing it in the flesh, huh?"

He strode over. Pure testosterone oozed from him. Had I really caused this? *Tut-tut,* I mused. *Must be more circumspect around rampant males.* I had to laugh. I couldn't believe he'd actually fought his way past Audrey and was standing right there inside the office.

"You better believe it. That performance was enough to drive a man insane." He knelt down and swung my chair round so it faced him. His eyes were green, bright green. I ran a finger over his stubbled chin. He captured it in one strong hand, giving me a look that announced he was taking control of the situation now.

"I had to get me a closer look," he added, and the smile he gave me was full of raw, undiluted sex appeal.

Before I knew what was happening, he'd grabbed my legs and hauled them apart. If I thought my little bout of exhibitionist self-pleasuring had been hot, I wasn't prepared for what came next.

He ran his hands down the inside of my thighs, feeling his way toward the hot niche at their juncture. He stripped my soaked G-string down my legs, manhandling me with ease. The way he looked at me where I was wet from pleasure sent a hot wave of self-awareness over me. Then I suddenly forgot how to be self-aware when the tip of his tongue found its way into the sticky, cloying heat of my slit and he was eating me up. I nearly lifted off the chair!

His tongue was agile and intuitive. He explored the territory of my sex before he began mouthing me, his tongue lapping against my swollen lips and over the jutting flesh of my clit. Rivers of sensation flew through my groin. My hands were knotting in his hair, my hips bucking against him. When he pushed an inquisitive finger inside me, I quickly came a second time, my body shuddering.

"Do you do this with every woman you meet courtesy of your squeegee?" I managed to ask, as I surfaced.

"Nope, most of them do a runner when I appear. Not you, though." He gave me that suggestive smile of his. He had one hand resting on his crotch, where he was rock hard inside his jeans. I was just contemplating how quickly I would hit the jackpot a third time if I had the pleasure of something that hard inside me, when I heard a sound.

"You're fired." It was Audrey. She stood in the doorway, her hands gripping onto the frame, glowering.

"Too late—I quit." Let's face it: It was only a matter of time before I walked out or got fired. It had been well worth it.

"I'm sorry," the guy whispered, one hand squeezing my thigh rather endearingly. He was genuinely concerned. What a sweetie.

"No problem, really. I was out of here, anyway." I leaned forward and pushed my fingers into his hair, hauling his head back. I kissed his mouth deep and hard, reveling in the sense of deviance that roared in my veins.

I glanced over just as Audrey staggered backward in the doorway, shocked to the core by my response, her mouth opening and closing like a fish's.

The man kneeling between my legs followed my gaze and chuckled low. "If you're looking for a new job, we need a receptionist at HQ. It's not a posh place like this, but we have a laugh. And it does mean I'd get to see you again."

His smile sent an after-tremor of pleasure right through me.

"Not to mention the fact that a chick like you would be a hell of a lot more fun than the dragon they sent us from the agency."

"You reckon?" I asked, pushing him onto the floor on his back, straddling him and reaching for his belt.

"I reckon," he said, grinning widely when he felt my hand reach for his cock.

What was the old saying about being in the right place at the right time and grabbing opportunities when they come by? My hand tightened on his cock. It looked like office work wasn't going to be so bad after all.

RED LIGHT, GREEN LIGHT

Shanna Germain

The room is small, more like a storage space with a huge front window. Right now, it's hidden from the street by a red velvet curtain. Another curtain divides this space—which holds only a tall wooden chair and a mirror—from the rest, which has a bed, another chair, another mirror, and a table with a lamp. The air smells like sex and old silk flowers. But everything's clean—nicer than I expected—with fresh sheets and clean floors.

I wonder how much Danny had to fork over to rent this window. I hope it wasn't more than a hundred euros or so, especially since I'm not likely to make the money back for him. I know if I asked him, he'd just shake his head and say, "You should never ask how much a gift cost, Luce." He'd run a hand through my blond hair, give my earlobe a tug. "That's why it's a gift."

It's a gift I've been wanting since Danny and I came to Amsterdam the first time, almost five years ago. Since the first time we walked these red-rimmed streets, hand in hand, watching the women in their rented windows. Some knocked on the glass at the men going by, others put their lipstick on in little mirrors, as though they were sitting alone in their bedrooms, oblivious to the men roving the street. Men swept by us, their hungry eyes on the windows, on the women in their string bikinis and high heels. "I want that," I'd whispered, tugging on Danny's hand, never daring to believe that he'd understand what I was asking. Never daring to believe that he would deliver.

Now, I grab a handful of the heavy curtain and peel it back just enough to see onto the street. The district's famous red lights are already out and twinkling, even though the sky is still an evening gray. A window directly across the way is already open. Behind it, a leggy woman with a black bob sits on a chair just like mine, her legs crossed demurely, her chest barely covered by a slip of fabric. Against the black light, her white skin looks mushroom pale, the fabric a ghostly green. Already, men crowd around her window. The backs of their heads are bathed in red light.

I look for Danny, but I don't see him. I know he's watching from somewhere. That was part of the gift. That he would watch. That he would let me see him watching.

It's nearly time. I go into the back room to strip off my jeans and sweater. I don't know why—it's not like anyone can see through the curtain in the front room. Maybe I just need this one final moment of privacy before I put my body in that window for everyone to see. It's been eight years of marriage since anyone besides Danny has seen my body. Now, I feel like the whole world will.

I slide into the maroon lace panties and corset—another gift from Danny—and slip on my highest black heels. I take a peek at myself in the mirror. The glass is old, and my face wavers in the uneven surface. But it gives me a good idea of how I look. Long, blond hair down around my shoulders, dark-red fabric contrasting with my pale skin and my nipples trying to press through little holes in the lace. I let my breath out in a rush and run my hand down my belly. It's flat when I'm standing, but I have no idea how it will look when I'm sitting down.

In the front room, the chair is hard, cold wood beneath me. I sit up straight, cross my legs, and put the black toe of my shoe against the window ledge. I take a deep breath, let it out slowly, and pull open the curtain.

Almost instantly, there are faces in front of the window. Men of all ages and colors. Eyes and eyes. I feel like a fish or a mermaid. Some press their fingertips against the window, leaving dirty smears. Others mouth things at me. English and Spanish and a billion other languages. *Cunt. How much? Fuck you.* I am so grateful for the glass between us. I skim their red-lit faces, looking for Danny, but I still don't see him.

Some of the boys are obviously from the States—Yankees caps and jackets that say UCLA and CORNELL. I skim over their pale faces. They're cute, but they're not what I want. With others, it's hard to tell. Black men with dreadlocks and knit caps, pale older men in sharp suits and leaning on canes. The few women walk hand in hand, looking either uncomfortable or excited.

One man stops in front of my window—young, shoulder-length blond hair. He looks for a moment, passes on, perhaps to something more exotic, something darker or skinnier. Next to these exotic women, I look very American. Or maybe very German, with my blond hair, green eyes, and come-hither hips. These other women, they have boobs the size of Texas. Not me—I'm all ass and hip and nipple. You could look all night, in all these windows, and not find the same body shape twice, I think. I could look all night into this street and not find the same man twice.

Another man, this one "armied-out" in a crew cut and broad shoulders, steps through the crowd, up to the corner of my window. He knocks, hard enough to make the glass tremble. I shake my head. He steps back through the crowd.

I watch the street. I'll know when it's right. I've practiced my wink, my rap-rap on the glass with the back of my knuckles.

When I see him, he's already looking at me. Watching. He's got olive skin and dark, heavy eyebrows. Tall. A dark wool coat that looks like it was tailored just for him. He's alone, despite the packs of men moving around him. When I catch his eye, he doesn't hang his head. Those brown eyes look right into me, as if he's appraising a piece of art, as though he's been careful to choose just the right piece.

I almost look down at the ground. Almost.

Instead, I breathe in the scent of silk through my nose, let the corners of my lips curve up. I duck my head just a little but keep my eyes on this man. I wink, and for some reason, I tap my toe against the glass, even though I know he can't see it.

He grins—beautiful double dimples on each cheek that send a shiver through my stomach—and takes a step forward. That's when I see Danny behind him, leaning against the railing that lines the canal. Watching me. The man is moving toward my window, but I keep my eyes on Danny, his grin barely visible in the red neon, while I draw the curtain.

I open the door and there he is, the man I've chosen, smelling of snow and wind and the doughnut shops that are on every corner. The cold air makes my nipples strain against the fabric.

"Yes?" he says.

I nod. I am afraid to answer, sure that my American accent will give me away as nonnative, that he will walk out the door before I have the chance to touch him.

He steps inside and I close the door behind him.

He takes off his coat, hangs it on the hook near the door. Beneath, he is dressed in an eggplant-purple, button-up shirt and black dress pants. "How much?" he says in English. His accent is almost hidden and is hard to place. Portuguese, maybe. Or Italian.

I'm tempted to offer him a freebie, since I'm just posing and, although he doesn't know it, he's actually doing me the service. But he looks like he has the money, and I don't want him to feel like he's not getting the real deal. Plus, if I'm going to do this, I want to do it all the way.

I put one hand on his shoulder. Cock my hip near his. "How long?" I ask. When I speak, he looks up from his wallet. I think that he is surprised by my accent, that he will ask if I am from the States.

Instead, he touches his cold finger to my bottom lip. Pulls it away from my teeth, pinching the skin gently. Lets his dark eyes linger on my chest, on my belly, on the front of my panties. Says, "One hour, maybe longer."

Despite the cold he's brought with him, my cheeks burn. "Fifty euros for twenty minutes," I say around his finger.

He nods, drops his hand away from my lips. I step in front of him, careful in my heels, and lead him into the back room, holding the curtain aside so he can follow. He is a big man in this small room, his shoulders wide through the doorway, and I am glad I wore my heels, glad that I can reach his shoulder without stretching.

I am not sure what do now. It was easy to play the seductress behind the glass, but here in this room that's so obviously made for only one thing, I am suddenly uncomfortable, like I don't know what to do with my hands. I haven't touched anyone's body but Danny's for so long—I know what he likes and doesn't—how do I touch someone new, let him touch me?

But then the man steps up behind me, cups my ass with his cold hands. The cool feels good against my overheated skin. The way his fingers grasp with want makes me less nervous.

I turn toward him, letting his hands stay around my ass, and reach up to undo his shirt buttons. Beneath the fabric, his skin is even and tight, the muscles across his chest strong. I slide the shirt over his shoulders, press myself against him. He pulls me toward him with both hands so that I can feel his erection, pressing hard against my belly.

"Lie down," he says. I lie on the bed on my back, and he lowers himself on me, running his tongue across my skin, nipping here and there with his teeth—the side of my hip, the tip of my nipple, the bottom of my lip. By the time he has his tongue against the front of my panties, my nervousness has changed to charged desire. My skin tingles everywhere. Even through the fabric, his tongue is sending quivers down my thighs.

I grab his head, pull it away from me. "Let me," I say. He lies down on the bed, and I slide his pants down. His blue boxer-briefs bulge in the front. A drop of precome wets the fabric. I run my tongue against the rough cotton. His liquid tastes like oysters and laundry soap.

He moans and lifts his thin hips, letting me pull the briefs down. His cock springs up, thinner and longer than Danny's, curving toward me. I climb onto him and rub my hand across the top of his wet head, down over the crown. He bucks beneath me, raising us both off the bed. I explore his cock with my hand: the small blue veins, the mushroom head, the way it jumps when I wrap my fingers around the base.

His hands wander over my breasts, tweaking my nipples through the lace bra, sending sparks everywhere. When I lean my head back and moan, he sits up, takes my shoulders in his hands, and gently pushes me off of him.

"Stand up," he says.

I do. He sits on the edge of the bed and spins me around until I am facing the wall. The room is small enough that I can lean my hands against the wall without moving my feet, my ass, away from the bed. I am breathing hard, my hair down over my face. He kicks my heels apart with his feet, nips at my ass. I can feel the small points of his teeth all the way up in my nipples, all the way down into the juices that soak my panties.

As though he can read my mind, he tucks the length of his finger right against me, right against the wet strip of cotton. Turns it over and over like a screw. I want to grind against him, but I hold myself still, hands on the wall, waiting to see what he wants.

He grabs the strip of fabric between my thighs, shoves it to one side. His finger inside me, cold and hard, makes my knees tremble, makes me cry out. With his other hand, he reaches around and pulls down the cup of the lace bra until my nipple's exposed. He pinches my nipple and pulls. It feels so good, I have to grind against him, get him to sink his fingers deeper.

When he drops his hands, away from me and out of me, I can breathe again. The crinkle of a condom. Then, "Sit," and he's pulling me down on him. His cock slides into me so smooth and fast that I can't believe it's happening and then it is—I'm fucking this stranger.

I ride him backward, his hand pulling me down, hips pumping up. I put my hand to my wet clit, think of Danny standing out there in the cold, watching my closed curtain, waiting while this other man fucks me. It nearly makes me come right there, just thinking of that. But I promised Danny I'd wait, that I'd wait for him. I have to take my hand away from my clit, concentrate on the man beneath me, on the way he moans and rocks under me, on the way his cock feels, longer inside me, as though he's reaching farther up in me than Danny ever does.

Soon, he flips me around so I'm facing him. He puts his hands on my ass, pulling him me onto him again and again. How different inside me, the way his hips move and his cock. I run my hands over his chest, the muscles moving, the way his chest hair uncurls under my fingers.

And then he's rising inside me, nearly lifting me off his hips. The muscle in his jaw clenches, releases. He cries out, his fingers tightening on my ass as he shudders and shakes and goes silent. I wait until he stops shaking, and then I wrap my fingers around the bottom of the condom and slide off of him.

I look at the clock by the bed. "One hundred euros," I say, all business. And then I go into the front room, with my dripping panties and my nipples aching, and sit in my tall chair waiting for him to get dressed and go.

When I hear him put the money on the table and shut the door, I slide the red curtain back open and look out into the street. The man in the wool coat steps out the door, stands on the concrete for a moment, men milling around him. He looks content, smiling like a man who's just spent his money wisely.

Danny leans against the railing against the canal, watching my face. He also looks like a man who's spent his money wisely. The man walks by Danny, nods his chin. My husband nods back. Two men passing in the street, two men who appreciate the finer things in life.

I look at my husband, at his handsome face, the gray hairs that I can't see but that I know are there, just above his ears. I stretch out my long legs, giving him a flash of nipple above the corset. Then I wink.

Danny pushes himself off the railing, comes forward, toward

the door that leads into my window. I slide the curtain closed one last time and walk to the door.

"How much?" Danny asks. He smells like coffee and my favorite shampoo.

"Everything," I say. "Everything you got."

THE CORNERS OF MY EYES

Stan Kent

When you've been as dedicated a voyeur for as long as I have you tend to think you've seen it all. Of course, that doesn't stop me from looking. I'm always searching for that elusive new scopophiliac thrill. But in general, the sexual events under my microscope do play out like an old favorite movie where you know all the words and every scene, but still watch, captivated, to the feel-good end, even though there are no surprises. Yet do not think that familiarity breeds voyeuristic contempt; while those moments where I catch my girlfriend Lizzie in flagrante delicto with some wannabe paramour on the dance floor are not new, watching her flirt, kiss, and fondle—and be fondled and sometimes fucked—always provides me with a luscious stiffening and a desire to fuck her senseless once we get home. Or perhaps in the nightclub's bathroom. Or in the parking lot. Or, oh, fuck it, right there on the dance floor. I may be a voyeur, but in the face of some serious sexy watching I become a doer.

As you might imagine, it's not easy being the object of my

eyes' affection. When going out there is an unsaid pressure on a voyeur's partner to perform. I realize it is tough to always be on your game, to feel like every night out is showtime on the center stage of my perverse passion play. I know, believe me, I know it is tough to come up with some new visual treat. I do appreciate the effort Lizzie goes to, hunting through her closets to find just the right combination of revealing clothes and fuck-me shoes, topping that off with the appropriate hairdo and makeup that will make the evening perfect. Don't get me wrong, Lizzie is a born exhibitionist and loves dressing up and showing off, but even stars crave their moments out of the public (or private) eye. Yet necessity is the motherfucker of invention, and what Lizzie came up with the last time we went out was a very mischievous way for us to have our voyeuristic cake and eat it, too. Just when I thought I had seen it all, the old familiar movie had a new ending.

That night, Lizzie looked particularly ravishing and especially ready to perform. Her burgundy wraparound miniskirt was split up the side and made of a semitransparent material that showed every curvaceous nuance, including the line of her pink thong and the bulge of her pussy lips that the panties barely covered. Her legs were sheathed in Wolford purple fishnet thigh-highs. Her feet were adorned in black, open-toed Christian Louboutin platform stilettos with wraparound ankle straps. She topped the exotic ensemble off with a burgundy corset laced up tight with the suspender straps dangling free. Her raven dark hair, streaked with tinges of copper and gold, fell about her bare shoulders. Her makeup, though perfectly applied, with the added touch of extra-large glittery eyelashes, begged to be messed up.

We arrived at The Eye, a new club in Hollywood, around eleven. From years of voyeuristic practice I've become skilled at scoping a nightclub from the moment I cross the velvet rope.

I scan for the vantage points where I can watch Lizzie be both predator and prey. I often feel like David Bowie in *The Hunger* where he and fellow vampire Catherine Deneuve prowl the second-floor gallery of a nightclub to the tune of "Bela Lugosi's Dead," surveying the dance floor for their midnight bite. Let me tell you, there is nothing more exciting than going into a nightclub as a loving couple, then splitting up into singles-on-the-hunt, knowing that at the end of the night we'll be back between each other's thighs. It's all the fun of dating without the messy, disappointing downsides faced by normal people: We never go home alone. And that's just one of the liberating benefits of being an exhibitionist/voyeuristic nonmonogamous couple.

It's ideal if there is a raised area where I can lurk in the shadows, single malt in hand, or perhaps a Sapphire and tonic, and stake out Lizzie being single. Tonight The Eye rewarded me with a comfortable booth on a mezzanine above the dance floor and bar. I was hard as a stripper's pole just sitting there in anticipation.

It never takes long for Lizzie to attract an admirer. She saunters onto the dance floor, drink in hand, and moves and sways to her own sexy beat, no matter what is playing. She radiates carnal heat, taking the occasional sip of her cocktail as if she must to keep cool. Okay, call me biased, but she can be on a dance floor full of other women and the guys fixate on her. She stands out not just because she has such sexy beauty and wears to-die-for-a-fuck outfits, but because she's there on her own, dressed to thrill. Guys simply can't believe their luck; women that beautiful and that seductively attired aren't usually available out there solo, roaming free like some tasty sheep in the midst of a hungry wolf pack.

I watch, wondering who will figure this lonely beautiful woman is just too good an opportunity to pass up and make a move on her. I know her type well; it's easy to predict the rejects. Jocks and frat-boy types need not apply. She goes for the exotic-esoteric type, although sometimes she'll toy with someone completely out of her wish list just to mess with me. She's knows I'm up there watching, and she knows that I'm turned on, and this is her way of letting me know she's in total control. It's funny when you've been together as long as we have—six years—we might be separated by a nightclub expanse, but we know each other's sexual predilections and what we're thinking as if we were next to each other comparing notes.

Tonight, Lizzie stayed true to type. After a couple of guys that looked like young Republican lawyers on ethics leave were dispatched to nightclub purgatory, Lizzie let a rocker dude enter her space. He resembled one of those countless lead singers of a soon-to-be-the-next-big-thing band who forever frequent Hollywood clubs waiting to be adored by some pretty young things, and whose pants are tight enough to show all the pretty young things his big thing.

Lizzie and Next Big Thing danced; they danced closer, bodies brushing. They kissed, and they retired to the bar. They shared cocktails. They felt each other out with conversation. They kissed some more. His hand slipped to her ass. At some point he asked for her number. She told him she had a boyfriend, but she was allowed to play around as long as he could watch. I may not have heard the exact exchange of words, but I've watched this scene unfold so many times that I can get the gist of what's being said from their body language. Next Big Thing's eyebrows arched and he smiled and nodded. This was a crucial point in the flirtation. If Next Big Thing bolted, then he was a no-confidence, insecure, vanilla, poser-rocker guy and not worthy of any more of Lizzie's favors. If he stayed, then he was up for some kinky fun.

Next Big Thing stayed, but just as long as it took him to finish his drink. I was surprised and more than a little bit let down. I thought he was made of sterner, kinkier stuff. I was looking forward to seeing him between Lizzie's widespread thighs. Before he left, they exchanged phone numbers, poking their respective digits directly into their cell phones. He gave Lizzie a kiss that was much more than just a friendly-see-you-later peck, and with a wave he was off. Lizzie finished her drink and signaled to me. I joined her. We danced, and I was entranced to be at the center of her universe again. We kissed with a passion that surprised me. It was deep, pleased-to-fuck-you lip sex. Our bodies ground together as we had sex with our clothes on, and when we parted for air I asked her about Next Big Thing. She liked him. He was cute and sexy and kissed good and possessed a nice-size cock she wouldn't have minded peeling out of his tight jeans. She was bummed he had split; he said there was a friend's band he had to go see play. He asked her to go with him, but she wasn't up for being a groupie, so they exchanged numbers for maybe another time when he wasn't so busy being a rock star wannabe.

After a few more unfruitful but fun solo encounters followed by more clothed sex we headed home. The promise of extreme sex hung heavy in the car. All the frottage had me extra horny. So was Lizzie. Her dance-floor tryst with Next Big Thing had steamed her into an all-hot-and-bothered condition. I can tell she wanted him in a bad way. The chance encounter and his escape had supercharged her libido for me to enjoy, and watching it all transpire had turned my sex drive way past maximum safe limits. These are the wonderful mutual benefits of our win-win–fuck-fuck relationship. It doesn't matter what happened on any given night out, because whatever happened always excited us into a frenzy that can only be satisfied by wall-to-wall fucking. Our scopophiliac soirées were all foreplay for our fuckplay, whether actual fuckplay with others was involved or not.

We were no sooner home and up the stairs when Lizzie pushed me down on the bed and stripped me naked while she kept all of her clothes on. She was rabid, tearing off my clothes, scattering buttons like ejaculate. There was a definite take-charge attitude about her that screamed she'd had enough foreplay tonight. I expected to be fucking like triple-X porn stars paid by the orgasm, but Lizzie turned out to be in an extra-playful, teasing mood. She used my skinny tie to attach one of my hands to the bedpost. She used my belt to tie the other. She stood above me, legs spread, stiletto heels nipping at my skin. She pulled aside her pink thong.

"Like what you see?"

"I always like what I see up your skirt."

"My panties are all wet. I'm all wet because of him. This is from him to you."

She reached under her skirt and slid the panties off her bottom. She dropped them on my face. I spoke through the mask, every breath catching the perfume of Lizzie's musky wetness.

"You wanted to fuck him, didn't you?"

"It would have been interesting."

"I'd have liked to watch you fuck him."

"I know you would. You always want to see me fuck someone."

She reached down and untied one stiletto and then the other, taking her time, making me savor the unshoeing moment, keeping her legs tensed and straight. She smoothed the thigh-high fishnets off her legs, treating me to a striptease. She squatted down on my chest. I felt the wetness of her cunt on my skin. She leaned forward and kissed me through her cast-off thong, her tongue working the wet panties into my mouth until I was well and truly gagged.

Lizzie then took the fishnets and wrapped them several times around my head until I was partially blindfolded by the mesh. It was torture, not able to see everything, but such exquisite pleasure to catch glimpses out of the corners of my eyes as I moved my head to angle the fishnets for a peek-a-boo view. It was a chase to see every little detail that I could, and lo and behold, in a few seconds of scanning I realized that Lizzie had come up with something new in my kingdom of voyeurism. My cock strained. How I do love this woman.

"You're wicked," I mumbled through the balled-up thong, but Lizzie couldn't understand panty-speak and did not want to hear. She ignored my pulsing erection and went for my nipples. Warning: I have sensitive nipples. They feel like direct, mainline extensions of my cockhead. She licked, twisted, bit, and flicked my nipples into sensitized bullets about to explode from the barrel of my chest. Once she'd tenderized my flesh with her fingers, she popped her boobs out of the corset and rubbed her nipples on mine, and then she sat astride me and rubbed her clit on my nipples. I was on nipple overload, somewhere between screaming, laughing, and crying. My cock pulsed and bobbed around, but she never touched it. She just worked my nipples over as if they were my solitary sex organ. I relished tantalizing glimpses through the purple fishnets of her toying with me. The constrained view added a layer of excitement to the touch that was hard to contain and explain. I thrashed, my head darting from side to side, up and down, as I fought for a clear view of Lizzie in action. It was a new watching thrill to be so close and yet so far from my reward. I was a wild man. I fought against the bonds so much that Lizzie chastised my unruliness and used my shirt and trousers to tie my legs to the foot of the bed. Now, I was well and truly spread-eagled. I figured this was the immediate prelude to a damn fine fucking, but it wasn't. She didn't. She flicked my cock with her finger so my erection slapped against my belly, leaving a strand of precome on my skin, and then she got up from the bed and walked to the door.

"Where are you going?" I thong-mumbled in disappointment, but Lizzie didn't respond. Out of the corners of my eyes I watched her take her sweet time in donning the stilettos, making a production of flexing her long legs, showing me her ass and pussy under her skirt before strutting away. In my partially sensory deprived state every sound was amplified above the thunderous roar of my pounding heart. I heard her heels click around the floor and down the stairs. I heard her pour a drink. I heard her put the glass down on the table. I heard the front door open and close. I heard silence. My eyes flitted around our bedroom, trying to make out details. I looked for the clock to get a sense of how much time had passed, but it was out of my fishnetted view. It could have been minutes or maybe an hour, it was hard to tell. But finally I heard the door open, followed by the familiar click of Lizzie's heels on the stairs.

And then I heard the not-so-familiar footfall of another pair of feet.

My heart raced as Lizzie entered the room, and I heard a man's voice follow her in.

"Oh, wow, is he all right?"

Through my fishnet mask I recognized the tight-jeaned crotch at the foot of the bed. It was Next Big Thing.

Lizzie laughed.

"Oh, yeah. I told you he likes this. He likes to watch, and this is a special treat I've cooked up for him."

"Oh, wow. This is weird."

"Are you okay with it? You said you liked it kinky. You sure you don't mind fucking me on the same bed?"

"Nah, I just don't want to be tied up like that. And I don't do dudes."

"Oh, don't worry, I want all your limbs and appendages free just for me."

Lizzie and Next Big Thing kissed at the foot of the bed. I watched her hands explore his body until I lost sight of her caresses. Then I saw his hands lift up her skirt and massage Lizzie's butt, pulling apart her cheeks as he pulled her to him, offering me a fleeting vision of her perfect, heart-shaped ass and puckered rosebud before he pushed her down on the bed. I felt Lizzie's hair fall over my legs. She sat up and unbuckled his pants, pushing them down, freeing his namesake, and yes, from what I saw, it was the Next Big Thing. Lizzie fondled his cock and kissed it, but the soon-to-be-fuckers didn't keep still, moving in and out of my vision. Far from frustrating me, the now-you-see-it-now-you-don't fishnet teasing only served to boost my excitement through the sexosphere out to where no man has boldly gone before. What I couldn't see through the mesh, I could hear and feel and thereby imagine as their bodies moved through what I was sure was a glorious cocksucking.

I felt the brush of Lizzie's skin as she slid farther up the bed. I sensed the curve of her hip against mine as she spread her legs for him. Through tiny purple frames I saw Next Big Thing bend to kiss her pussy, and as his tongue made contact, Lizzie grabbed my bound hand and squeezed my fingers. Her head rolled from side to side. Her legs bent upward, opening her cunt wide for Next Big Thing to lick and probe. Lizzie's hand slipped from mine and flopped on to my chest where she played with my sensitized nipples, squeezing hard in sympathy to the attentions Next Big Thing lavished upon her clit. We thrashed together, separate on the same bed, linked by our shared desires to see each other's needs satisfied.

I know I've said it before, but I can't help gushing. It's not every day or night that a voyeur's eyes are opened by having them partially covered. This was a new kind of voyeurism for me, involving all the senses, with much more mystery and imagination than would have been required if I'd been free to observe and even participate. It was like being in a sexy dream where not everything is visible and all things seem possible. Despite Lizzie's touching me, and my reactions, they acted as if I weren't there. More so, I believe, than if I'd been free to join them. I was just like another piece of bedroom furniture to fuck against.

Next Big Thing rolled Lizzie onto her stomach and tongued her ass. She kissed me on the lips, pulling the thong gag from my mouth. Her tongue wrestled mine in a deep, desperate kiss. Her face partially obscured my view of his face buried between her callipygian buttocks, his arms wrapped around her thighs, feasting on her treats. Lizzie broke our lip-lock and whispered in my ear.

"He's good. This is good, isn't it?"

"It's very good. It's so different. I can only see so much, but I feel it all. You are very good."

"No, I'm very bad."

Lizzie's words morphed into an extended moan as she pulled away onto all fours to reveal Next Big Thing fucking her from the rear. He held her thighs and pulled her into him, and the bed rocked under me with each thrust, making the fishnetted vignettes of their sex blurry and tantalizing. It was impossible to follow as positions switched. I was the only constant, spread-eagled as Lizzie and Next Big Thing's fucking tossed them around the bed. I felt their bodies clamoring for each other, brushing against me as I saw flashes of their body parts entwined.

Lizzie ended up on top of Next Big Thing. She took his cock, slapping it on her clit before sliding it into her pussy, looking at me as she did so. She blew me a kiss as she ground her pussy into his crotch, rocking backward and forward, working her clit. Next Big Thing lifted into her, and as Lizzie swung her arms out she brushed against my cock. Her fingers wrapped around my shaft, and as she fucked him she stroked my cock. I'd been on the verge of coming ever since Lizzie's nipple torture had left me in a sensitized state. Her velvety grip on my cock was all that I needed to erupt into her hands. Next Big Thing was also on a hair trigger. He let out the kind of throaty yell you'd expect from a wannabe lead singer, pulling on Lizzie's nipples as he came, making her bounce up and down on his come-sensitized cock, bringing her off as she continued jerking my come-sensitized cock past my blinding release, elevating us all into a state of delicious delirium.

As Lizzie's breathing settled and she came down from her orgasmic high, she pulled the fishnets from my head and mopped the come from my chest with my see-through-blindfold stockings. As I calmed down, she leaned forward and kissed me, and then she leaned over and kissed Next Big Thing. From my completely clear vision I could tell the kiss was not so much a passionate one as a thanks-for-the-fuck-now-it's-time-to-get-your-gear-on-and-go peck. As Lizzie and I kissed and cuddled, Next Big Thing must have concluded that he'd fulfilled his role, so he did just what Lizzie's kiss had suggested.

He paused in the doorway.

"See ya."

Lizzie shook her head.

"I don't think so, but I will see you out."

Naked Lizzie showed Next Big Thing down the stairs and out through the front door. There was minimal conversation and what sounded like a brief kiss goodnight. She ran up the stairs and leaped on the bed.

"Everything cool?" I asked.

"Yeah," Lizzie said as she untied my bonds. "He understood that you're the only one who gets to really see me, even if it is out of the fishnet-covered corners of your eyes."

INTERVIEW WITH A PORN STAR

Radclyffe

"How can you fuck strangers for a living while people stand around and watch?"

That's the question everyone *wants* to ask me, although most people try to sound more polite. Sometimes, I hate doing interviews because no one ever believes my answer. It's too simple, I guess. The truth is, acting in erotic videos is the perfect job for me because I never have to fake coming, and you can always tell when a girl is faking it. Of course, when I say that, they either look really, really skeptical or say, "How can you come when it's *all* fake?"

Sigh. Like girls can't get off just like guys for no other reason than it feels good?

Then I have to explain that there is nothing fake about having a girl lick your pussy or stroke your clit and that I get off on people watching her do it. Having sex in front of other people makes me come like nothing else. Oh, I get off plenty of other ways and it's always good, but I never come as hard as I do when I know someone else is looking. So the minute I walk onto the set, even if the director and the cameraman and the sound techs aren't standing around the bed yet, my pussy gets wet. Put me with another actor in a roomful of people watching us fuck or go down on each other, and my biggest challenge is *not* coming before I get through the scene. I still have to concentrate on holding off until the director wants a come shot, but I've been working on that ever since the day I completely embarrassed myself at my first film audition.

I didn't know what to expect, so I was psyched when it turned out the director was a hot woman. That was the first plus for me. The second, even better bonus was that she was looking for an actor to make it with other girls. I have nothing against guys, but girls really do it for me. There's nothing quite like a pouty mouth slick with lipstick cinched around my clit, unless it's a small, hard fist pounding inside my cunt. Besides, girls look so sexy when they come. It doesn't matter if I'm fucking them or sucking on their hot, hard clits or watching them do themselves, I love the way their mouths open with surprise and their eyelids flutter and their bellies quiver just before they cry and throw their heads back and gush all over.

Oh, yeah, I like to watch almost as much as I like to be watched. Almost.

So I told the director I was good with the girl action, and we got through the age thing and the health thing and all the other routine stuff pretty fast. Then she put the paperwork aside and stood up.

"Do you mind if I take some stills for the website? I like to feature our new actors before the film release."

"Sure. That's fine."

"Right this way." She led me into an adjoining room that was set up like a photography studio. Except this one had a big bed right in the middle of the room. We were the only ones there.

"Go ahead and take your clothes off. Then stretch out on your back on the bed."

While I got comfortable against a pile of big fluffy pillows, she fiddled with the equipment.

"Let's run through the basics," she said as she walked to the foot of the bed with her camera. "Are you comfortable masturbating in front of other people?"

I almost laughed. I first discovered I *really* liked people to watch me come when my housemate walked in on me one afternoon while I was masturbating to a porn video. She wasn't supposed to be home for another two hours, and when the front door opened and she strolled in, I was like thirty seconds from coming. My clit had done that thing where it plumps up right before I pop, and little electric shocks were running through it into my stomach and down the insides of my legs. The girls on the screen were sucking each other's pussies, and the way their mouths sounded on each others' cunts—wet and slippery and yummy—had me rubbing my clit as hard and fast as I could. I turned my head when I heard the door and saw her and my orgasm stalled just before I hit the top, but my cunt was so swollen and achy I couldn't let go. She looked at the TV and then at me, her gaze zeroing in on my skirt hiked up to my waist and my hands working between my legs.

"You're home early." I gave her a lazy smile and slow-stroked my clit, my fingers coated in juice.

"Sorry," she said, but she didn't look sorry. Her eyes were huge, and I could see her breathing fast from across the room; her nipples were hard little balls under her tight T-shirt.

"It's okay," I murmured breathlessly. "But do you mind if I finish? I really need to come."

"No, I don't mind," she said so quietly that I almost didn't hear her. "Could I... Could I watch?"

The look on her face, so hungry and helpless, made my hips jump and, oh, God, I was on the edge again, every bit of blood and bone and muscle coiled so tight it felt like my clit would explode any second. And it was so good, I knew I'd come really hard, even harder than when I was about to come from watching the movie.

"Sit next to me." I circled my clit as softly as I could so I wouldn't come right then, but I really, really wanted to.

She just about ran across the room, but she didn't sit on the sofa like I expected. She knelt on the floor between my knees, put her hands on the inside of my thighs, and leaned over until her face was a few inches from cunt.

"You like it?" I asked, flicking at my clit.

"Oh, yes."

I spread myself open with the hand that wasn't teasing my clit so she could see everything. "Tell me."

"You're all red and puffy," she whispered. She looked up at me briefly, her face filled with wonder. "Have you been doing this long?"

I nodded, my stomach clenched so hard I could barely talk. Having her see how excited my pussy was made it open and close like a fist. God, I wanted to just let go all over her. "Almost an hour."

"Oh," she breathed, refocusing on my pussy. "You must have to come so bad now."

"Uh-huh," I whimpered, rolling my clit between my fingers. Across the room one of the girls on the screen was wailing and thrashing and rubbing her pussy all over the other girl's face. Usually that's when I come, watching her face twist and listening to her cry and mauling my clit until I force my cunt to spasm and flood. But not today. Today, I'd found something so much better. "Can you see my clit?"

"Yes, it's beautiful. So big and shiny." Her eyes were hazy and unfocused, like she was stoned, but I knew she wasn't. She was high on the smell of my cunt and the squelch of my fingers sliding through it and the sight of my stiff, wet clit. "Does your pussy feel good when you rub it like that?"

"Good, so good. Can you tell how hard my clit is?"

"Oh, yeah. It's sticking way out, and the more you tease it the darker it gets."

I moaned and circled the head of my clit. Watching her lick her lips and blink rapidly while she followed my fingers was making my pussy spasm, and I knew I didn't have much time left. "I'm going to come soon."

"Can I play with myself?"

"Do you want to come up here and watch the movie?" I held my breath, almost afraid of what she might say.

"Oh, no." She shook her head vehemently. "No. I want to watch your come spurt out on your fingers."

My legs jerked and I couldn't hold back a tiny come. I moaned and clamped my fingers tightly around my clit, preventing the rest of the explosion. "Go ahead. Play with your clit."

She yanked her zipper down and shoved her hand into her jeans. Even though her body convulsed, she never looked away from my fingers. I was still squeezing as hard as I could, afraid if I stroked even once I would come all over the place.

"Hurry," I whispered, "if you want to come with me."

The cords in her neck stood out as she shook her head again. "Watching you come will make me come." She looked up at me, her eyes glazed. "Your pussy is so beautiful, so open and wet."

My clit couldn't get any harder, and I rubbed it faster, big sweeping circles reaching as far down as my opening and then back up over the top, sliding the hood down and over the head with each swipe. "Watch my clit," I gasped. "I'm going to come."

She whined and pumped her arm faster, mumbling, "Please come, please come, please come."

"Here I come," I cried, pushing down hard as my cunt pulsed like a small heart.

And I did. She put her face closer but didn't touch me, and my hips jumped, and I gushed over her lips and her chin and her neck while her eyes rolled back in her head and she came with her hand digging in her jeans. Then she sweetly licked me clean while I watched the girls on the screen and came again.

After that, we got off together a couple of times a week. She especially liked to crouch between my legs in the shower and hold me open with both hands while I hit my clit with a stream of water from the shower massage. The whole time I was making myself come, leaning against the wall on trembling legs, she described the way my pussy jumped under her fingers and how my clit stood out from my body and how the rivulets of come ran down my legs and mixed with the water in pearly strands. She could predict the exact second when I got ready to come from the size of my clit and the color of my pussy.

"Oh, yeah, you're gonna come. Right. *Now.*"

And the minute she said it, I'd let loose all over. Then she'd suck on my clit while it was still hard, before I was even totally done coming, and bring herself off in her hand. While she was moaning and coming and mouthing my clit, I'd come again, too.

It got so all she had to say was, "Let me see your pretty pussy," and I'd be ready to come. So, no, I didn't have any trouble working myself off in front of other people. I loved it.

"I'm comfortable with public masturbation," I told the director, hoping to sound professional.

"Good. Let's take a look at you."

I spread my legs, and as soon as she looked down, I felt my

pussy swell. I'd shaved so everything would show for the camera, so I couldn't hide a thing.

"Hold yourself open for me," she said, adjusting a portable light so that it bathed my lower body in hot, bright light. "Use both hands."

I felt a trickle of come slip down between my cheeks. I hope she didn't see my fingers tremble as I pulled my outer lips apart. I knew from masturbating with a mirror how my cunt looked when I was excited—how my lips got thick and red and wet and my clit got long and fat. She must have been able to tell how turned on I was because she glanced up at my face and smiled.

"Looks like you're doing okay."

"Yes, fine," I said casually while my clit twitched and got stiffer by the second.

Click.

I imagined the way my pussy would look in the photograph, open and glistening with come.

Click.

My big pink clit, stiff and exposed, shamelessly aroused.

Click.

I started panting.

"Your cunt's a great rose color. That will look terrific on film."

Every click of the camera was a caress. My stomach started to hurt. I wanted to come.

"Can you touch your clit a little like you were going to masturbate? I want a shot of that gorgeous clit."

"Okay," I whispered, almost choking on the word.

Click.

I pressed two fingers on the base of my clit. It jumped right up and my belly rolled.

"Work it up just a little more. It looks fabulous when it's erect."

Click.

"Now pull the hood back and get it wet."

I painted my clit with come, and that made me so horny all I wanted was for this to end so I could go somewhere and finish myself off.

Click.

"Oh, that's a nice look. Jiggle it a little so it plumps up."

I did, and it was so good, and I should have stopped but I couldn't and I came. I tried to hide it, but it hit me so fast my whole body jerked off the bed. "Ooo! God!"

"Do you always come that quickly?" she said, clicking away while my pussy pumped.

I shook my head no, whimpering pathetically, still pulling at my clit and coming.

She lowered her camera. "Just really worked up over the audition?"

"I think," I gasped. "I think it's... Oh, God, this is embarrassing..."

"Hardly. You're perfect, but I still need to know what set you off so I can time the come shots in the scenes. Unless you can hide it a whole lot better than this."

"I can't...not usually," I confessed, thoroughly humiliated. "I come hard."

"Then I need to know your trigger."

"It's you looking at me. At my pussy."

"You get off on having people admire that beautiful cunt of yours?"

"Yes."

She laughed. "Oh, baby, you're going to love this job."

She had no idea and neither did I. I'm easy to pick out in the films—I'm the girl smiling right at the camera and coming, so nice.

OPERATOR 84

Thomas S. Roche

It's a long ride, as the crow flies, from Tribeca to the Upper West Side. But traffic's next to nothing at four in the morning—even on Saturday night.

We've been dancing in one of those exclusive clubs—you know, the one you like so much. You always get turned on when you're dancing. You always get really turned on.

Maybe that's why you can't wait.

Or maybe it's because we've stumbled upon one of those rare New York fixtures—the female cab driver. Instead of grunting at us and talking about politics, traffic, or the weather, she asks us in a musical voice, "Where can I take you?"

There's plenty of room in the backseat, but you snuggle up against me, your body lithe in its tight little black dress. You lean back and kiss me.

"Tenth and Seventy-seventh," I tell the driver. Smiling, I add, "And make it snappy!"

"You've been reading too many detective novels," she says,

smirking a little. She's somewhere in her mid-twenties, probably a student. She's got long blond hair and pretty eyes, which she disguises with a Yankees cap pulled down indelicately over her face. "Been dancing?"

By then, you've started to snug up your black dress and reach under it. I look down at you with my eyes wide; I want to ask you what you're doing, but I sense instinctively, from knowing you so well, that nothing is going to stop you—so I may as well enjoy the ride.

"Yeah," I tell the driver. "We've been dancing."

Your lacy thong comes smoothly down your thighs, over your ankles. You kick off your flats and tuck your panties into the pocket of my dress slacks.

"Lots of great dancing down in Tribeca nowadays," says the cab driver, looking at me in the rearview mirror. I can see the side of her face, and she's smiling; she's got a bright, enticing smile, and I spend about five seconds trying to figure out whether she knows what's going on. "Yup, the neighborhood's really bouncing back."

"Uh-huh," I say as you reach for my cock. "Bouncing."

By then, you've slid down behind the seat and you're kneeling between my legs. Knowing better than to argue with you, of course, I spread them enough to give you access.

"Yeah," I say, my breath coming short as your hand closes around the rapidly growing bulge in my pants. "There's nothing quite as great as a night dancing." I swallow nervously as you make short work of my belt and pants, apparently not caring if the driver recognizes the telltale jingle of my belt buckle, the revealing sound of my zipper going down.

"Sure," she says. "Dancing's great. Getting all sweaty. All those bodies pressed in against yours..." She utters a girlish giggle, something I never expected to hear from a cab driver of any gender. "Meet anyone interesting?"

Your lips descend on my hard cock, sliding down effortlessly as your tongue works against the underside. I have a lot of difficulty speaking at this point, but I manage to carry on the conversation. "Oh, well, you know," I croak. "My wife and I... We weren't really there to meet people. Just to...dance."

"With each other," she says, turning to look at me and smile as the cab comes to a stop in traffic.

"Yeah," I say, as your mouth works its magic on my cock. "With each other."

"I can tell. Does your wife like dancing?"

My cock slips out of your mouth. "Oh, yeah," you say from between my legs, slurping a little as you lick your lips. "I love to dance."

For a moment, I'm afraid the cab driver's going to lean over the seat and look down, but she doesn't. Instead, she turns back around and hits the gas, giving your mouth on my cock a unique sort of gravity as you slowly pump my hardness in and out. I'm having trouble now, struggling not to moan as the cab driver talks about how much she loves dancing.

"I love wearing something really sexy when I'm dancing," she says, glancing back to smile at me. "I can't dress sexy with my job, obviously. So I really like to doll up when I go to a club."

Now you've pulled my pants all the way down; they're around my ankles and your mouth is on my balls. "Oh, really," I say, my throat tight with the effort of speaking. "What do you like to wear?"

"Oh, you know, something like what your wife is wearing." She glances back again, her eyes dark with mystery. "Where'd she go, anyway?"

"Oh, I think she's asleep," I murmur. "She had a bit to drink at the club."

"I bet. I guess there's no reason to stop now."

My ears ring as I realize, without a doubt, that she knows what's going on. But both of us maintain the pretense, even as you take the hint and climb up into my lap—facing me.

"Yup, there's something very sexy about getting dressed up to go dancing," the cab driver says as you take my spit-slick cock in your hand and guide it to the entrance of your pussy. The cab driver looks back at us. "Oh, I'm sorry, am I distracting you?"

You moan softly as you settle down on top of me, my cock deep inside you. You slump forward against me, heavily, and your hips start grinding in that way you do, barely moving but causing almost more friction than I can take. You know how to make me come—but, more important, you know how to make yourself come, and your hand is wedged tightly between our bodies, rubbing your clit.

"Of course, wearing something like what your wife is wearing, I can't wear much under it. I mean, when it's tight, you know, you get panty lines. I have to go with a little tiny thong. Do you find that, too?"

She glances over her shoulder, pretending not to notice that you're grinding on top of me, kissing me hard as you drive my cock rhythmically into your pussy.

"Yeah," you moan softly. "Sometimes I don't wear anything at all."

She giggles, turning back to the road. "Me, neither," she says. "Of course, I didn't want to say that, but sometimes I just go with nothing on under my dress. Saves time later."

"Yeah," you say. "Oh, God... Saves time..."

I can tell you're going to come, and now we're clear of the midtown traffic, hurtling down Eighth Avenue at a breakneck pace. It's almost like the cab driver is in competition with us, trying to see if she can get us where we're going before we can finish. But you're quick as a wink with that hand on your clit, and you don't try to camouflage your moans when you come. Your body presses hard against mine, your hips pumping rapidly, and you moan loudly, throwing back your head and whispering "Oh, yes, oh, yes, oh, yes..."

Which is when I come, my hips working my cock up into you, your smooth thighs pressing against mine. I'm not quite as loud as you, but any notion that the cab driver is clueless is long since gone. I clutch you tight and kiss your neck as my orgasm dwindles.

When I open my eyes, I see that the driver is turned around in her seat, her legs tucked under her. She's watching us—openly, shamelessly.

"Here we are," she says.

You slide off of me, my cock slipping out of you. I reach for my pants and start to pull them up, groping for my wallet as I do.

"How much do I owe you?" I ask, my face reddening.

"Oh, look at this," the driver says. "I forgot to turn on the meter. Well, we'll just call it even."

"Thanks," I say as you smile at her and get out of the cab.

"Operator eighty-four," she says, smiling as she hands me a card. "I work Fridays and Saturdays." She's taken off the Yankees cap, and I can see her pretty eyes flashing under the streetlights. She turns back around and puts the cab in gear.

"Next time, though, don't expect the ride to be free."

GLINT

Portia Da Costa

"What the hell *is* that?"

There it goes again...that flash of light from the cottage on the headland. Is it what I think it is? Is someone up there spying on us with binoculars?

"Whassup?" grunts Gavin from beneath the towel he's got plonked over his face to keep the sun out of his eyes. I'm surprised he even heard me over the football commentary on the radio. I thought he was totally tuned in to the European Cup. I didn't think he was actually paying attention to me at all, but it seems he is.

"Nothing... I'm not sure... I just keep seeing a flash of light or something from that cottage up there."

Suddenly, I'm reluctant to admit my suspicions. They're pretty stupid, after all. People stare out to sea with binoculars all the time. There's nothing to say that whoever's in the cottage is looking at us, if, indeed, they are using binoculars. It could just be sunlight glinting off a windowpane that's flexing in the heat.

"Right," Gavin mutters, reaching down to idly adjust himself in his trunks while at the same time turning the radio up with his other hand.

Git! He wasn't really listening after all…

If Gavin had his way, we'd be back at our own cottage and he'd be in front of the telly, watching his precious football instead of just listening to it. Me, I could fancy a bit of steamy, sweaty afternoon nookie—but Gavin, in typical lad mode, seems to be satisfied for the moment with a few beers and the beautiful game.

But it's our first seaside holiday together, and it's the sunniest day since we got here, so I've insisted we hit the beach, football or no football. To give him credit, Gavin accepted this with good grace

Ack, there it goes again! That glint of light…

What are you looking at, you horrible perv? There's nothing going on down here for you to lech and wank over… Would that there were!

I'm not really complaining. There's actually been plenty of sex since we arrived at the cottage and plenty of orgasms. But it's all been pretty basic stuff, if you know what I mean. Missionary, routine foreplay, the odd bit of oral… Satisfying, and almost throat-catchingly tender at moments, but just missing that indefinable something in the thrills department. No adventure. No spice. No Factor X.

Nothing daring and kinky like doing it in public while someone watches through binoculars.

What the hell is the matter with me? Where did that come from?

I ought to be outraged at the thought of somebody spying on me while Gavin and I are making love, but the idea's got into my head now, and I've a feeling it's stuck there. Instead of tilting the parasol so that our distant watcher—or watchers—can't see us, I get up, take hold of it, and twist it around out of the way so it doesn't obstruct their view. And while I'm up here, I lift my arms and do a sort of supermodel thing, pushing my hair back from my face in a way that makes my boobs rise in my bikini top and salute the sun.

Get a load of that, whoever you are, I challenge, running my hands down my neck and my shoulders and then down the sides of my breasts. Lingeringly and lovingly, as if I really fancy myself... It's a shame there isn't more of an audience, actually, but there's only me and Gavin here on the sand this afternoon. This is a more or less private beach for the little cluster of cottages that hug shallow cliff top and the edge of the band of dunes to the west of it. You can't get down here by road, so there's no passing trade, and we've got this pretty expanse of pearly sand all to ourselves.

"What're you doing, love?"

I jump and spin around, and find Gavin has shed the facial towel and is watching me, hands behind the back of his head and eyes narrowed against the sun. Which is a great pity, because his eyes are one of his finest features—brown as brandy and very deep and dark and sexy.

"Oh, just looking around...getting the lay of the land and all that."

"Okeydokey, then," he observes placidly, not really all that interested after all. "Just watch out for the Peeping Toms, won't you?" He's suddenly got that look on his face that indicates he's already elsewhere, despite the sight of my skimpy bikini and my rather less skimpy body. The announcer is working up quite a head of steam now, waxing lyrical about a corner awarded and there being plenty of bodies in the box. Gavin's eyes close again, and the towel goes back on.

Again... *Git!*

I can't really be cross at him for long, though.

He's quite a hunk, my Gavin. Tall, big-built, and yet almost pretty despite his size with his sexy boyish face, his snub nose, and his dark, curly hair. When the football's not on, he's actually quite fantastic. Caring. Attentive. Thoughtful. As well as being intelligent, well informed, and lots of fun.

Yeah, you up in the cottage...take a look at me in my tiny bikini and my fabulous boyfriend with his smashing body and his great big dick inside his swim trunks.

The more I think about this, the hotter I get. And not just from the sun. Kneeling down on the rug, I snag my bottle of Factor 30 and spin off the top. I slop far more than I need into the palms of my hands and then begin to smooth it slowly and luxuriantly over my face, my shoulders, and my arms.

I close my eyes and imagine the person up in the cottage watching me, eyes wide open. Whoever they are, they're watching with longing as I caress myself, or maybe as Gavin wakes up and starts to help me slather on the suntan lotion. As he gets bolder and slips off my bra top, there's a sigh of approval from the watcher.

It's all so real to me that I suddenly realize I'm wet inside my bikini bottoms and my nipples are standing out like little wine corks and rubbing the inside of the bra cups of my top.

"Oh, to hell with it! I'm going topless!"

The towel flies off again. "What about the bloke in the cottage up there?"

The football is forgotten. Or it's halftime or something. To my surprise, Gavin's switched off the radio.

"Fuck him! If there is a him." I unclip my top and fling it away across our beach rug.

"You'd better get some lotion on those," announces Gavin

cheerfully, coming up on his knees and reaching for the sun lotion bottle. "Don't want to burn your gorgeous titties, do we?"

As he straightens again, I notice something else has come up, too.

Gavin has big hands, but they're very deft and clever. He's a computer engineer—although not a geeky one—and he handles the tiniest and most fragile components with perfect ease. Much the way his lotion-greased fingers are handling my boobs now. Circling round and round, making sure the Factor 30 coats them thoroughly, thumbs slithering over my nipples again and again, again and again…

And still, in my mind, we have an audience. The watcher is getting aroused, too, even though I don't know if it's a man or a woman. Maybe it's a couple? I imagine them at their window, passing the field glasses from one to the other. The one who's watching masturbates one-handed, while the other one makes do with an unaugmented view and uses both hands to give himself, herself pleasure.

Gavin is breathing heavily now, really getting into it, squeezing my breasts almost roughly.

It makes me feel objectified and slutty but as hot as hell.

"I think they're done now," I gasp, wanting him, oh, God, wanting him to move on to other zones.

"Yeah, right," he gasps, and as I look up into his eyes, they're almost black with lust and gleaming like metal. He grabs up the lotion bottle and pours a great double handful. "Let me do your back…and your front… Turn round a bit."

When I've wriggled out of my bikini pants, his hands assail me, back and front, just as he said. One settles on my bottom, sliding and palpating, and the other inveigles its way into my pussy, fingers going straight for my clit.

This isn't basic. This isn't routine. This is incredible. Gavin kneads and rubs me, his fingers working hard, but just how I want them to, slicking sun lotion in and amongst my juices, almost working them up into a satin froth. I shake and buck, jerking my hips back and forth, but he never misses a beat, never strays off target. I throw my hands around his neck, leaning against his big, powerful body as he manipulates me, and pressing my thigh against the bulk of his meaty erection. It's swollen so big now that it's poking up out of the top of his trunks, the head slippery and wet with his silky precome.

"Oh, baby," he purrs vaguely, still paddling at me and rubbing himself against me as his fingers work, "You're so hot... It's no wonder people watch you. I bet that bastard up there is wanking himself stupid right now, wishing he was me, down here, touching you."

Oh, oh, God, that's it!

I come like a runaway train, my body convulsing, grabbing at empty air until Gavin sticks a finger inside me. It was the thought of the watcher that did it. The idea of hot eyes devouring the sight of us rubbing each other and smearing ourselves against each other in a sticky, sex-mad muddle down here on the sand.

Take a good look, you freak! Or freaks! I call out silently, even as my body goes again, climaxing again on top of my first climax, my fingers gouging deep into the solid muscle of Gavin's broad shoulders.

There's only one thing I want more now than to have some distant perv watching me orgasm with my boyfriend's hands on my pussy and my bottom, and that's to have my big, beautiful boyfriend's big, beautiful dick inside me.

"Oh, love, I want to fuck you," groans Gavin, reading my mind.

I whimper as his hands retreat, but then start to murmur

encouragements again as he lets me down onto the blanket and almost tears off his trunks. For a moment, he fumbles around in his beach bag, and then he's ripping the foil off a condom—which does make me wonder whether football was all he had on his mind this afternoon, after all. He wouldn't have come prepared, otherwise, would he?

Naughty Gavin!

And then he's on me and in me, his great gorgeous length hammering me against the hard-packed sand beneath the blanket while my legs wave and kick, out of control. He feels ten times bigger than normal—even though his normal size is pretty fabulous—and I know it's because he likes the idea of being watched just as much as I do.

Is this what you wanted to see, you perverts? The two of us, going at it on a public beach? Well, take a good look! Take a good look and wish you were here with us!

It's too much...just too much! I come again, shouting now, howling and writhing and clutching at Gavin, my hands slipping and sliding on his oily back, my ankles hooked around the back of his knees to jam myself against him like a reciprocating engine.

And Gavin's right here with me. He shouts like a bull, goes rigid, then pumps and pumps and pumps at me in an orgasm that seems to go on forever.

I glance toward the cottage, and the sunlight glints again.

THE CRAZIEST THING

Gwen Masters

The craziest thing I've ever done? You really want to know about that? Well...I'm not sure it was crazy, but it was damn well necessary. Oh, yes. It was.

Does it have anything to do with my boyfriend? What do you think? Of course! Have you ever known anybody as crazy as he is? He's an absolute nut. Sometimes he proves it. He sure did that night. There are other stories, but that one takes the cake.

I'm getting to it! Good grief. Let me rest a minute and tell this on my own time.

Being a musician's woman is hard work. All my friends used to think it was so glamorous, traveling to all these different cities and meeting all sorts of people. And it *is* glamorous at times, to have a popular singer for a boyfriend. I admit that I still get a bit of a tingle when I hear him on the radio. Yes, after all this time. How silly is that?

The money? Well, there's lots of that, too. Let's just say that a performer might get pennies for his records, but concert tickets are another story, and he's selling them out nowadays. But that's not what I love about him. He could live in a cardboard box and I would still love him. I like to think so, anyway.

Sometimes, I still have to remind myself that this isn't a dream. Even with all the travel and hard work and bad food and lack of sleep, it's worth it to be with him. What isn't fun is the way the groupies hang all over him. I'm a jealous person by nature, and a jealous person's choice for a significant other probably shouldn't be a man who shakes his ass on stage for screaming women on a regular basis. However, you can't choose who you fall in love with, isn't that right? And that's okay. Being with him is worth the gnawing that my jealous bone takes every once in a while.

The crazy part? As if that much isn't crazy enough. I'm getting to it.

On this particular evening I was waiting backstage, watching my man say hello to a variety of fans before boarding the bus for the next town. Adam was quickly becoming one of the hottest singers in the business, and it was evident by the dozens of screaming women waiting for his bus early in the morning, hoping to catch a glimpse of him—or more—before he started sound check.

I watched Adam work the crowd in the way only he can, signing autographs and making everyone feel welcome and special. He paid a bit too much attention to that little blond slut who had been lusting after him in the front row—she was right there beside him, moving closer and closer as she talked to him about how wonderful she thought he was. Of course, he always had a thing for blondes, and I knew that. He didn't try to hide it, and how could he? Never mind that I'm not a blonde. I teased him about it until he asked me to dye my hair.

Sorry...you're right. Stick to the story. Good grief, you act like you're horny or something!

Adam kept casting a wary eye at me, not sure what to expect from me. I had learned long ago to take all this in stride, but like I said before, sometimes the jealous bone begins to ache. This one couldn't have been more than twenty, probably younger, with bleached hair and enormous breasts that couldn't possibly be real. I quirked an eyebrow at Adam, and he grinned back. He had dealt with her kind before.

Adam was just being the nice guy he is, you know. But she was moving closer. Her breasts brushed his chest. Before anybody realized what was coming, she rose on tiptoe and slid her tongue into his mouth.

Oh, yes, she did! Can you believe the audacity of that bitch? I was stunned.

What did I think I would do if this moment ever came? I knew it could happen. I just never expected it to happen in front of me! Adam wasn't kissing her back, mind you. Being a friendly guy had quickly turned into something much more serious than what he expected.

What did I want to do? I wanted to kick her ass! But security was pulling her away, and Adam was blushing like mad, and I didn't want to make a scene among those fans who were already so curious about me as it was.

So I spun on my heel and ran for the bus. Damned if I was going to stay there! I had seen enough. A town that size had to have a cab company. I could make it to the airport and wait there for Adam to head out of town.

Then Adam's footsteps were loud behind me. He caught me halfway to the bus, grabbing my arm and spinning me around. He said, "Baby, I'm sorry. I didn't kiss her back. Where are you going?"

"I'm so tired of this shit!" I hollered as I yanked my arm away from him. Why was I mad at him? Oh, hell. I wasn't mad at him. Not really. I just needed somebody to take my anger out on, and he was convenient.

"But I'm yours," Adam said with a plaintive tone, as if that solved the entire problem.

"I just wish they knew it," I said. I admit I was playing the victim card. We had been over and over this whole conversation a million times.

So then Adam said, "Let's show them."

That stopped whatever I was going to say next. He had to be kidding. And I was not amused. I asked him what in the world he was thinking, what in the world he was talking about, did he really think that I would buy a suggestion like that as being the real deal?

Adam shut me up with a kiss. A good, deep, rowdy kiss, the kind that made my knees weak. He whispered against my lips, "I'm dead serious. Try me and see."

I couldn't believe this. He was actually suggesting it! There must have been fifty people there in the parking lot, watching us.

Waiting.

Adam's cock was already pressing hard against me through his jeans. I heard someone laugh, then a murmur rose from the crowd as he bent his head and kissed me again, this time with even more passion than before. I felt my resistance melting away.

When I opened my eyes, I saw the slut who had kissed him only a few minutes earlier. She glared at me. Yes, she did. That fucking bitch. Just thinking about her now, all this time later? It still pisses me the fuck off.

I slid my hands down his back, and he tensed up, then laughed a little into my mouth as his tongue danced across mine. Did he think I would go through with it? Probably not, but the realization dawned on him soon enough. Every part of my body was primed and ready, and like all longtime lovers, he knew it instinctively.

I pinned my eyes on that bleached whore on the edge of the crowd.

"He's mine," I said. I was loud enough that everybody could hear. "Wanna see?"

One person laughed, and another yelled encouragement. A few people left, but most stayed, jockeying for a better position. Adam grabbed my shirt with both hands and lifted it over my head. The cool breeze fluttered over my tight nipples and made me shiver. Or maybe it wasn't the breeze. Maybe it was the fact that we were being watched.

Let's see how the tabloids write about this one!

Adam's mouth moved down and his tongue reached out to flick my nipple. The crowd was getting louder because everyone now realized what was going on. The whore who had kissed my man was standing there with a furious look on her face, so I gave her a big smile. She turned on her heel and stalked away, and I felt more than a little haughty as she left. Victory was mine!

Adam's knee slid between my legs and pressed high. I wanted him, right here, right now, right here on this asphalt. Apparently, Adam wanted it as badly as I did, for he picked me up and carried me a few feet to an old Oldsmobile and settled me onto the hood. He wasn't all that gentle, let me tell you. He unzipped my pants and pulled them off. Fast, like a teenager wanting to fuck before his mama gets home. My sandals came off with my jeans.

It wasn't until then that I realized I was naked. In front of a crowd. It's funny how things sneak up on you in the heat of the moment.

Adam yanked his shirt over his head and smiled down at me as he unbuttoned his fly. His hard cock sprang out, fully erect and ready. I heard the groupies begin to make noise, moaning and talking in low whispers about my man. He smiled down at me as if there were no one else around, then reached for me.

His first touch sent me arching high on the hood of the car, my blood throbbing as he slid one finger gently into my wet pussy. He leaned over me, shielding me somewhat from prying eyes.

"Are you sure this is what you want? You sure you want to fuck me right here in front of everybody?" he asked me while his hand began a slow rhythm, thrusting against my cunt. A second finger joined the first, and his thumb flicked across my clit. God, he knew just how to get me going. I spread my legs for him and sensed the crowd closing in, watching every move.

Adam was always the showman, even at a time like that. Maybe especially at a time that. What man wouldn't be? He stood and hollered, "Y'all enjoyin' this?" He was rewarded with a roar of approval as he knelt above me, sliding me up the car so that he could join me. My head rested on the windshield, and I vaguely heard the door open and some of the crowd slide into it for a better vantage point. Figures, huh? I didn't care at that point, because Adam had moved down and spread my legs wide, burying his face between my thighs.

You're not embarrassed, are you? This is what you wanted to hear, wasn't it?

The first touch of his tongue made me groan. The crowd pressed closer in appreciation. Then his hand joined his mouth, and I found myself perilously close to the point of no return. I opened my eyes again to see a group of men and women pressing near the car, their eyes riveted on me. Some of the men had unzipped their pants and were stroking their hard cocks as they watched. Others were being sucked off by their girlfriends or wives. That was interesting, seeing other people get hot enough to fuck just because I was hot enough to fuck. Talk about a power trip!

Adam closed his lips over my clit and sucked firm and gentle, the way he knew I liked. I went off like a rocket. Yes, right in front of all those people. Swear to God. Yeah, *I* was shocked, too.

The crowd roared. The sound was dull in my ears.

When my body calmed down, I looked up to see Adam above me, his cock poised, its swollen head just barely touching me. His smile was slow and gentle, but the fire in his eyes said he was almost gone.

"Let's give them the show they came for," he suggested, and I smirked back at him, swiveling my hips in invitation. I was enjoying every delicious minute.

"Should I give it to her?" he hollered, and the group hollered right back in assent.

"Does she deserve it?" he asked, and they said, "Oh, yes."

"You wanna see me fuck her?" he taunted, and the crowd began to beg.

Adam linked his fingers with mine and thrust in, plunging to the hilt with one fluid motion. I was shocked by how aroused he was. He groaned and buried his head in my shoulder for a moment before he reared back to give the crowd a good look at our joined bodies. I looked down and watched along with them as he pulled out slowly, his cock glistening with my juices, then slid back in just as slowly, making sure everyone could see. A collective groan rose from the crowd, echoing my own.

Adam was harder than I had ever felt him. He fucked me slowly, holding back as best he could, his thighs tense with the need to slam into me as hard as we could both stand it.

Did I come again? Oh, yes. I certainly did. But it was the mind fuck that was so damn good. The psychological high of doing it in front of so many people and the thrill of staking my claim. Whoever said men were territorial had obviously never met a jealous woman!

Anyway, then it was Adam's turn. He braced his hands on the windshield behind me and slammed home, his hips driving hard, pumping in and out of me with a viciousness that made me gasp and cling to his shoulders. He rammed me like a hammer driving a nail, and I wrapped my legs around his thighs and then his hips, pulling him close and forcing him as deep as he could go.

Meanwhile, the crowd was having its own fun. A few men were doing the same thing Adam was, slamming into their lovers with a fire fueled by voyeurism. A few were jacking off right there near the car, watching Adam go at me like a raging bull. Of course, many of the groupies were getting off, too—there were also those who just stood there in envy, wishing they were in my place. Those bitches were practically green!

I met Adam thrust for thrust, reveling as his cock pounded me harder than he ever had before. It hurt like hell, honestly. But was I going to show anything other than sheer excitement and lust in front of those groupies? Hell, no. Especially not when Adam pulled back and slammed deep, holding there while he lifted my legs over his shoulders.

The crowd went wild. They whooped and hollered while they watched our impromptu rodeo. Adam drove deep. That position and his angle meant that he got as deep as he could go, and I took a real battering that night. My pussy burned as he fucked me. I knew he was getting close, because his eyes drifted closed and his breath became short and his motion got a little jerky. You just know, you know? He was going to come.

"Let me have it, Adam!" I whispered into his ear. "Let them see you explode for me."

Adam groaned and thrust one last time. He began to erupt

inside me, the way I liked it, his cock spurting thickly into my pussy. He pulled out to finish shooting his load on my thighs. The crowd cheered at the sight. Adam collapsed on top of me, and we rested for a moment while the crowd around us continued their fun. I looked over to watch a man come all over his wife, bellowing with the thrill. Another man came in his girlfriend's mouth. It was like a live porno. If anybody had a video camera that night, they got themselves one hell of a recording. No, I haven't seen it pop up on the Net yet, not like that Paris Hilton thing. But you never know.

Anyway, we lay there for a minute, and Adam suddenly chuckled. "I can't believe we just did that, can you?" he asked.

Well, no. I couldn't believe it. It was starting to sink in, the *oh-shit* factor. What had I done? Jesus. It was insane. It was... crazy. Yeah, that's the word. I guess it was crazy.

A very generous fan handed Adam his shirt and jeans without a trace of embarrassment. No one bothered to hand me my clothes. Yeah, I noticed. I also noticed the glares.

Somehow we got back to the bus. Yeah, the tabloids were vicious. They branded me a slut. A groupie, just like those dime-a-dozen whores. Even though they knew I wasn't those things, tabloids are meant to pull in a lot of money, you know? A slut on the cover is better than a fine, upstanding wife any day. They wore out reams of paper over our sexual escapades, but our engagement barely warranted a peep. Priorities, you know, and sex sells.

Anyway, that's my story. My crazy story. There have been many concerts since then. And the groupies increased in number after that, but they learned to have some respect for Adam. Some of them even respect me. How twisted is that, huh? I've heard rumors of him fucking around, but they are just that. Rumors. Remember that old showbiz adage: "Those who tell don't really know?" It's true. Adam is faithful to me. You know that and I know that. Let everybody else talk, because it doesn't matter anyway.

Some fans actually waited around for a replay at later shows, but we never sang that little number again in public. Not yet, anyway. But you know, one day another woman is going to have to be put back in her place when she goes after my man. I do have a jealous bone, remember?

Go ahead and laugh, smartass.

You love to hear all the juicy details, you know you do!

FOR ALL THE WORLD TO SEE

Matt Conklin

Christina is at her most beautiful when she looks as she does right now: eyes wide, mouth open, brown hair carelessly tossed around her face, waiting for me to do something—anything—to her. I'm standing in front of her while she's perched patiently on our couch, naked. I'm wearing brown cords and a light-blue, button-down shirt, but that doesn't really matter. I'm not looking at myself right now but at her staring back at me. She's waiting for me to tell her what to do, to slam her back against the couch or lift her up by her hair, to order her to spread her legs or turn over so I can spank her. I can tell her almost anything and she'll lap up my words, get off on hearing them spoken just for her. Her submission is written clearly across her face, the makeup she'd so carefully sported when we sat down to dinner two hours ago now largely worn away. Her lips are still wet and dark pink, but from being bitten, from her tongue sliding over them in trepidation and anticipation, not from any gloss. I watched her while I ate my dinner, let my eyes bore into her until she had to blush and look away. Even knowing each other as well as we do, I still wield the power to melt her simply with my eyes. The look on her face at this moment is one I want to remember forever, one I've captured in my photography studio but still never managed to fully do justice to. Right now she's quivering before me, live, for my eyes only, though she's too fucking gorgeous for me to be that selfish all the time.

I like to capture her with a click of the shutter when she doesn't know I'm watching—bent over the fridge searching for the milk, fresh from the shower, staring deep into her computer screen. She puts up with it because, deep down, she likes that I can capture a side of her she rarely sees when she looks in the mirror. But she knows that I also see something deeper, that when I push her to her limits, I see her masochistic soul laid bare.

"I want to suck your cock," she says with so much earnestness I know she means it all the way through. Her face contorts when she says it, the ache traveling all the way down to her cunt. I can see the effect the words alone have on her body. She doesn't need to lick her lips; I know she can practically taste my dick on her tongue. It twitches in my pants as I look at her, the silence extending between us as she waits for my response. My initial urge is to whip out my cock and immediately shove it into her open, warm, wet mouth, slam it deeply down her throat, pin her shoulder against the back of the couch and fuck that sweet, soft hole of hers until she's choking on me. I could, and she'd practically come right then and there from the invasion.

I know exactly how it would feel because I've done it before. When we first got together I literally could not wait and would have her naked within minutes of coming home with me, have her hands around my cock or my tongue deep inside her or her spread out before me while I slammed into her over and over. Back then, I'd barely had time to watch my cock disappear down her wide-open, eager throat, with nary a moment to register the beauty of those lips pressing against my shaft, her cheeks puffing out, the glorious, arousing struggle written across her scrunched forehead as she matched my thrusts with her own. She's never been the kind of girl who just lies there and takes it. Even tied up and almost immobilized, she makes sure I know she wants me, that she'll do anything to have me. I'm glad to be older and, hopefully, a little wiser, because the rewards for me of waiting are ones that only reveal themselves when I draw out the torture.

"You really want to suck my cock?" I ask. The more either of us says it, the more we both want it. The first time she said it I had to struggle to hide my shock. I'd been with girls who knew their way around a blow job before, but never ones who'd asked for it with such reverence, such passion, such need. Never a girl who trembled when she spoke, who asked with the slight fear that I might say no, that I might be the kind of guy who prefers girls on their backs than on their knees.

"Yes, Matt. I really want to suck your cock. I'll do anything if you let me take it between my lips." She whimpers then, and I slap her across the face. Not that hard, but hard enough to see the pink bloom on her rounded skin. She stops whimpering and looks up at me, the threat of tears lurking behind her eyes, her pale, pretty face lit up by the marks of my fingers. This she wouldn't ask for, but I know she wants more. I step closer, my erection clearly visible through my pants. She swallows, her eyes darting from my cock up to my face and back. She has her legs tucked under her almost daintily, as if she weren't a dirty, horny slut with a nipple ring and a desire to be smacked around and fucked so hard she screams. I pinch the other cheek, then run my thumb along her bottom lip. Her lips part, but I don't press it inside; I watch instead as her body unfolds into an even more willing posture. I push my thumb down the slight cleft in her chin and on to her neck, pressing just deeply enough to make its presence felt. She keeps her eyes locked on my face the entire time. I pinch her left nipple hard, twisting it between my fingers. The dark pink flattens as I twist it, and I pinch harder, waiting for the noise to go with what I'm seeing, the soundtrack to my sadism. Finally, after pressing even harder, harder than I'd planned, she lets herself indulge in a small tremor. I slap that breast, making sure her nipple meets my fingers as I do. All the senses I'm using converge at once—sight, touch, smell, hearing (taste will come later)—blending together as each touch makes her gasp, each pinch makes her redden, each word makes her musk that much stronger.

Christina keeps opening her mouth and then closing it, taking deep breaths that clearly precede something she wants to say but chooses not to. I like seeing that indecision splash across her features, like watching her struggle over what to ask me to do to her, never knowing if reverse psychology will get her what she wants, or straight-up begging. It's like she's physically handing me her power as those pink lips widen and shut, tears rushing to her eyes the longer I hold off making a decision on just how to defile her gorgeous body. The truth is, the cruelest thing I could do isn't hit her but ignore her, walk away like I don't need her just as much as she needs me.

I used to be the kind of top who worried about what my subs were thinking every second of our play. "Is that okay? Do you like that? What do you want?" I'd ask. In trying to be solicitous, I'd killed more moods than I cared to remember. I could see their bodies deflate, going from puffed up, proud, and perverted to sunken, shy, and stubborn. With Christina, thankfully, I know what she wants most of the time and can read her well enough to make educated guesses. I thrust my right knee between her legs, winnowing them apart, slamming the fabric up against her shaved, wet pussy, feeling its heat against the denim wall.

"Spread your legs and keep them spread," I say, and she does, maintaining the position with some effort. Her thighs tremble as she sits there with her sex spread before me, pink and beckoning. Again, my cock throbs with the need to be deep inside that other hole, my favorite, to press against those soft, pale thighs with my hands, as if holding her open for me, then sliding into that velvety tunnel. "Put your hands over your head and tilt your head back, Christina," I say. God, I want to take my clothes off, but I can't just yet. She's putting on too sexy of a show right here to bother with anything other than watching.

She does, her hands rising to reveal underarms marked by only the barest of stubble, triceps on the verge of becoming firm but still fleshy enough for my taste. I don't know where to start, because her whole body looks so tempting. Soon, I promise myself, I'll get to sink my cock between those lips, which are now gently parted, her eyes closed as she presents herself to me. I trace a finger along her slit, but she tries to close her legs to lock them around my arm. I swiftly remove my finger from her wetness and press her legs even farther apart. Christina lifts her head and looks up at me as I look at her cunt. I see the large, asymmetrical lips falling on either side, the promise only hinted at beneath. I push harder and see the strain in her thighs, the wetness beginning to leak as she fights to hold the pose for me. She doesn't mention my cock, but from the look on her face I know Christina is still dying to suck it. I use my knees to keep her legs open, leaning over her on the couch with one armed balanced on the back of it, the other resting against her neck. My lips are inches from hers as I look at her face, so much younger without glasses or makeup or armor of any kind.

I exert a light pressure against her neck, more a stroking than a squeezing, feeling her heart beat beneath my fingers. "How badly do you want to suck my cock, Christina?" I ask, then lift my hand to pry open her mouth, holding it for a few seconds while she struggles to swallow. When she doesn't answer the instant I take my fingers away, I grab her by the back of the hair, twisting her away from me, then tugging her back. Another slap across her cheek echoes through the room. "Do you really want my cock buried all the way down your throat? Do you think you can take it all? And even more importantly, do you think you deserve it?" We both know perfectly well that, in this state, she could probably stuff three cocks in her mouth, so horny is she, but I need to hear her say it as many times as it takes for her to break, to topple some of that greedy pride she holds so dear.

"Yes, I want it. I want to feel the tip against my tongue and then take all of your cock into my mouth. I need it, Matt—you know how badly I need it. I'll do anything," she says, more quietly than before. And that's when I get the idea for what will happen next. I'm still impatient, but thinking about the way she swallows my cock—the way her lips glide up and down and then somehow, in an instant, have it all the way inside—forms an image in my mind I know others will want to see as well. I've photographed her before, but stills can't compare to live, hardcore action.

"Come with me," I instruct, standing up and pinching both nipples for good measure before lifting her up from the couch. I carry her to my room but not to the bed. "Get on your knees right there and wait for me," I say, pointing directly in front of my computer...and my new webcam. I'd gotten it because my buddy Charles said it would be easy, and he'd been right. But thus far, considering I wasn't looking to get laid or flirt or any of the more traditional purposes, I hadn't seen fit to use it. But now I wanted to give someone, anyone, a chance to see what a good little cocksucker Christina was. And even though I like to watch a lot more than I like to be watched, I'm turned on by the idea of strangers seeing her swallowing my dick. I don't know why, I just am.

Christina looks up at me, her breasts sloping gently downward as she stares me with that same look of need across her face. I slap her again, and this time tears do spring to her eyes. "Matt, I need to suck your cock. Please just let me taste it," she begs, then gives a little sigh-moan that has me unbuckling my pants. She opens her mouth, unbidden, letting me look inside there, too. I pushed my pants off until I'm standing there in my briefs, my cock barely contained by the soft black cotton. I slap the other side of her face, just because I can, then lean down and kiss her.

"You like it when I hit you, don't you, Christina? Tell me the truth."

"Yes." She's shaking as she looks up at me, her eyes wild with my cock so close to her, pink blooming on her apple cheeks. "I want you to slap your cock across my face."

Either she really wants to suck my cock or she's trying to make me come in my pants because the dirtier the words that spill from her mouth, the more turned on I get. Maybe I've heard them before and maybe I haven't, but with her it doesn't matter. It always feels like the first time, like I'm spoiling some innocent girl who deep down just can't get enough, which isn't too inaccurate a description of my Christina. Outside this apartment, she's all "please" and "thank you," giving directions, tipping well, a good Samaritan. But with me, she's a slut par excellence, and if I didn't give her what she needs, I know she'd leave me for someone who could. Good thing we're a match made in crazy, kinky heaven.

"Close your eyes," I tell her, and she does, but with a look that tells me she doesn't want to. I know she likes to watch for as long as she can, likes to see my cock up close, likes to flutter her eyes open when she's swallowed the entire thing and look up at me from down there, as if asking for approval. But I slip a small, black blindfold over her eyes so nobody will be able to tell it's her. As a reward, I let her lick the contour of my cock through the fabric. Her tongue immediately darts out to trace my hardness.

I tease her, holding her by her hair and peeling down my briefs so only the head is available to her touch. "Kiss it," I say, and dutifully, she does, her lips meeting my engorged flesh and almost making me cry out in a very unmanly whimper. "I'm going to let you suck my cock, Christina, but there's a catch. You're such a good little blow job giver that I think your talents could be appreciated by many rather than just little old me, so I'm going to put my cock and your mouth on my webcam so people can jerk off to the way you suck my cock. I bet lots of guys are going to wish they had you kneeling before them with that pretty little mouth just waiting to devour them, and they don't even know how fucking wet you are right now and how hard I'm going to fuck you after we're done with this. They don't know how I'm going to make you bend over with your hands on the ground in front of you, your palms and your feet flat on the floor while I fuck you the way you like it best, or how I'm gonna slap your ass while I do. They don't know how really dirty you are. They don't know anything about you and they don't have to. All they're gonna know is how greedy you are for my cock, how much of a pretty slut you are when you beg to have your mouth filled."

I shove two fingers into her pussy to make sure she's getting as turned on as I think she is, and she gasps, clutching my arm. I curl my fingers, then bring my thumb to her clit while I let her lean against me, taking great, heaving breaths as I bring her right to the brink of orgasm, then stop. "I guess you like the idea of the whole world watching you do what you do best, isn't that right?" I say. She raises herself back to her previous position and nods. My only regret is that I can't see her pretty brown eyes, can't see if they're fearful or excited or teary or alert. But the blindfold adds a whole new element of excitement. I'll be watching her as well as anyone who cares to, but she can't see any of us.

I step away and turn on the camera, and a close-up of her face looms on my screen. Then I step into the frame and see my cock, but it looks different in front of me—digitized, enhanced, slightly removed. I look away, giving that view to those who don't have a Christina in front of them, live, hungry, and horny. I slap her face with fingers still wet from her juices, then feed them to her, two and then three and then four. "Unnhh," she mumbles against my fingers, and I slide my briefs down with my free hand while fucking her mouth with the fingers of the other.

"I think you're almost ready for my cock, Christina. What do you think about that?" Her throat immediately opens wider, allowing me to press farther. And by then even I can't wait anymore. I pull my fingers out, then hold my cock out to her lips. She immediately starts devouring it, her hand reaching for the base to hold onto. I flick it back, then firmly place both hands behind her back while my cock shoves deep down her throat. "Keep your hands there; you don't need them to suck me," I tell her. She grunts her agreement and then starts doing what she's been begging for all night. She has ways of letting me know what she wants even without stating it, so by the time she'd asked so clearly earlier, I knew. I knew from the way she ate her food, slowly, the fork lingering in her mouth. I knew from the way she played with my fingers over dessert, tugging them and staring at them longingly that she needed this hole filled the most, that her throat needed to be filled with the gift only I can provide. Her mouth is a marvel, a miracle, as she slides back and forth along my length, sucking me sloppily, her body shaking with the effort to stay in control even as her insides are leaking all over, tears, saliva, pussy juice spilling forth as she rocks to and fro.

I'm so hard I feel like I might pop any minute, but I wait so I can fully appreciate the view. Her pink lips are wrapped around my pole, her invisible tongue gliding along the underside. She easily takes all of me into her, then stays there with her lips pressed up against the base, nuzzling the strands of hair strewn there, pushing farther, as if seeking some hidden treasure of cock she can unlock with the right pressure. I grab her, twining my fingers through her hair, and immediately she backs off a little. Even with the blindfold on I can see what this is doing to her, see how with Christina her mouth is just as sensitive as her pussy, the two connected in ways I don't always understand but appreciate nonetheless. I ease her head all the way back, then slam my cock into her mouth, sneaking a peek at the camera as I do.

"You're so beautiful like that," I tell her, and she smiles around my length, or tries to, the effort endearing and adorable as I let her explore my cock with just her lips and tongue and nose, one hand wrapped around a wrist behind her, struggling not to reach for my body to balance herself.

"Isn't she?" I ask the camera, leaning over to press a button to let it zoom in on her face for a moment before pulling back. Up close or from my vantage point, she's the most beautiful girl I've ever seen, reduced to raw need that's finally being met. She's left with only three senses by which to process what's happening, and she makes the most of them, her nostrils flaring as she breathes in my scent, rubs her face against my hot spear, licks long lines up and down, and then moves back to the head, which she paints in circle with her tongue.

I watch all of it, memorizing her pink, wet lips, the way the same cock I've held in my hand thousands of times looks completely different in this context. I don't pay too much attention to it when I'm jerking off. It's not that it's small or shabby by any means. But I don't have that need to stare at it as proudly as I do now, showing it off for unnamed viewers even as I show off my girl's most prized possession—her mouth. I hold my cock in my hand and, as she'd suggested, slap it across her face. Her tongue scrambles out eagerly, and I slap it with my cock, then beat it against her lips before plunging back inside. I hold my fingers around the skin at the base, pressing against my balls as she pushes forward to meet my digits, her soft lips kissing my knuckles as she swallows me again and again. The sound of her breathing is getting louder and louder, and I realize that as fun as it would be to do a real money shot and splatter her lips with my come, I need to fuck her more than I ever have. I almost lose it when she pulls off and says, "I love you, Matt." For her, this is not just about sex, not just about proving herself the best cocksucker I've ever encountered. It's about loving me, worshiping me with her mouth, with herself. I lean down and kiss her, my big tongue claiming her small mouth, then turn off the camera. She's all mine again.

"You're mine, you know that, right?" I ask as I slip off the blindfold. This time I do see tears streaking her face and they're gorgeous. I lick one cheek and then the other, tasting their saltiness. Up close like this, I see the tiny freckles that come and go with the sun, the faint marks and lines that you can only see from such a tight angle, the ones I really do think of as mine alone to view at my leisure.

"I'm yours," she says, keeping her eyes on mine even though

I know she wants to get to my cock again. I can't look away, and instead of what I'd planned, I put her on her back. Lifting her legs onto my shoulders, I rub my cock against her cunt, graze her clit with the head. She's so wet I can't hold off and I sink inside, leaning down so I'm crushing her breasts against my chest. I see her hair, now even more tousled, spread out before her, stray bits of glitter along her forehead—see the spots where her lips are chapped from overuse.

I reach my hand between our bodies and press against her clit hard with my thumb, then shift just so to that position that always make her look like she's about to pass out. I watch her face for the show that never gets old, no matter how many times I press REPEAT, the one that I feel in every inch of my body as the tunnel of her cunt tightens around me before the ecstasy takes over, the culmination of her night's work written all over her body as she looks up at me one last time with those big, brown eyes before letting herself sink into the bliss of orgasm. I pull back and then slam into her, plunging as deep inside as I can before pulling out and coming in a single stream of hot lava that has her twitching all over again. I lie down next to her and hug her as tightly as I can, letting her keep right on shuddering into my arms. This is the Christina I plan to marry, the girl who'll go where her deepest desires take her. Sometimes I want to share such beauty with the world, and sometimes I want to be the only one who gets to bask in what she offers up to me. Christina gives me the power to choose.

But no matter what, I get to watch.

THE ASTRONOMER

L.A. Mistral

1.

Thomas set the GPS and drift scanner and looked up at the night sky's dark, infinite body. All his friends were there: the Belt of Venus, the Whirlpool Galaxy, the Cocoon Nebula, Andromeda, and Bellatrix. The stars and the silty foam of star clusters gathered around him like old friends. The images stared back at him, crisp, stable, and so close he could reach out and touch them. For the third time this week, and about the same time every night, he scanned the southern horizon for luminous bodies.

He liked searching for luminous bodies at celestial distances. He took comfort in such distances. The space between distant solar systems shrank down from light years to an arm's length with the properties of his lenses and mirrors. He made a career scanning stars, but tonight something seemed different.

Something *was* different. Thomas felt another source of light in the firmament. He checked his star map, then turned the telescope right and left across the heavens. Nothing attracted his eye. He checked his star map again. He passed the telescope once again across the heavens. Thomas looked for anything different, anything unusual. There was nothing, so he scanned lower.

Her star-driven skin drew his attention. Thomas swung the telescope back.

He saw her luminous body rise on an apartment balcony. Light bounced off her into a spectrum of shimmering skin. Her blue eyes matched the vaporous atmosphere of Venus with its soft, blue atmosphere. Her eyes were almost amethyst in how they seemed to reflect green and gold. The long eye of the telescope brought him so close he could see the pores of her skin. They were as smooth and pale as the Mare Magellan or the moons of Titan. She wore mascara and had auburn hair and bedroom eyes. Her thighs were as flawless as the insides of almonds. She stared out of the apartment balcony, naked except for panties and high boots. She smoked like she was wondering about something.

Thomas backed away. He was accustomed to the distant intimacies of the rings of Saturn and of Dione, its smooth-bodied moon. Stars and planets were regular friends, steady and consistent, and it was no coincidence that he had taken up astronomy the same year his wife left him. Since then, he searched for consistency and connection at astronomical distances. The proximity of skin, however, was still an awkward intimacy.

The planets were mathematical in their regularity. He liked it that way. Sometimes he thought he was too predictable. He still preferred the immaculate distances between him and light. This woman drew him close, and he wanted to guard his anonymity against the fusions of her skin.

Thomas checked his watch. It was just after ten. He pressed into the soft rubber of the eyepiece. She appeared again, the same pose, still smoking. She was tempting him into her intimate properties. She welcomed him with her deep sighs and her inviting thighs.

She sang to him with her bedroom eyes, drowsy and tucked into satin sheets.

Her eyes dreamed the dream of ancient, star-invested voyages. She dropped the cigarette to the floor and looked right at him as she ground out the butt with the heel of her shoe.

"Just as I suspected," he said. "The brighter the body, the more it hides. Light is shy sometimes. It hides inside denser bodies."

He wondered if she would ever shine for him again.

2.

Thomas returned at ten the next night, but she wasn't there. Her balcony was dark, with no cigarette to guide his way to her. His other stellar friends had returned like recurring angels. He searched the area around Alpha Centauri, making calculations and photographs, and biding his time.

Just after eleven, Orion came out, and the woman came out at the same time. She was waiting there, leaning over the balcony with the inscrutable skin of Scorpio, wrapped in the thin air of her sighs. He roamed over her with his eight-inch telescope. The triangle between her legs was a shadow beneath her short, diaphanous robe. The geometry of her cunt was approachable, and he evoked her though his widest lens.

Thomas wondered if her husband or boyfriend would catch him. He was frightened that his neighbors might call the cops.

"Should I quit looking?" He thought to himself. "Am I trespassing on some inviolate space?"

He searched her face for clues, and she neither shivered against the opening of her balcony nor tightened herself against another's open gaze. She welcomed his ocular contacts, his

THE ASTRONOMER

visual caresses. His eye glided over her skin, like a satellite looking for other life. When he watched her, he magnified the vivid landscapes of her body.

His eye was a voyager, her silent companion.

Light is lonesome for light.

He rehearsed his innocence. He could always say he was stargazing, that he was an astronomer.

"Yes, that's it," he thought. He was a stargazer, a mystical astronomer, an alchemist of the flesh.

The more he looked, the more her body bloomed. The stars and her skin were equally public. Then she lifted her skirt in slow motion, almost to her waist, as slow as a sunrise. Her body swam in light. He was ready to commit sins to worship at her shrine.

"Revelations always involve risks," he thought.

He looked again, and she raised her finger as if to say, "Wait a minute," then disappeared. Thomas lifted his eye from the eyepiece and wiped his brow. Intimacy made him vulnerable, even at these distances. He leaned forward and nestled into the viewfinder again. The woman returned carrying cardboard. She wrote on it with lipstick the color of a warm breath in cool places. She wrote one word: SARA.

3.

The next night was just a short visit. His eye licked light off her smooth, extraterrestrial skin. He was a connoisseur of her particular light. Taste on the practiced palate of the retina. Her nipples were the size of nebulae. They were red, too, swollen with light. They lit his way to her. Her thighs peeked out pale and smooth. Light bounced off into the spectrum of her skin. Angles of color washed over her as if she were the shore on every star on this side of the galaxy. His eye loved the surface of things, her amethyst eyes, her extraterrestrial skin.

His eyes swam in her skin like swans.

She liked her watching him, and Thomas felt her eyes make slow pilgrimages over his body. He felt explored by curious eyes. He felt valued. It was like a private invasion, an insertion of her sight into his secret pact of silence and distance between them. She had breached his untouchable architecture.

He wondered if he should make a sign of his own.

"No," he thought. "Distance perfects intimacy."

The curtains stirred, and a shadow touched a shadow's hand. Thomas didn't know it if was the shade of the moon or the movement of a man. Then he saw the man himself, fully clothed and taking Sara fully by the waist. Sara pointed at Thomas.

The man looked directly at Thomas. He looked at the telescope, but Thomas was already gone.

4.

Thomas couldn't visit Sara the next night. Maybe he didn't want to see her. He was startled by the man; besides, he had to lecture on "Mythology of the Autumn Sky" to an evening class of undergraduates. He brought slides of Pegasus, Herakles, Achilles, and Andromeda. He wove tales of the thirst for gold gone unquenched and of love thrown away. He told the history of stargazing, heavenly exploration, and human tragedy. All the while he was thinking about Sara's slightly parted lips, the palpable trajectory of her throat, and the revelatory text of her eyelids.

The following night, she appeared again, naked to the waist. Her nipples were the size of nebulae. Her breasts luminous beings, still lit up from the original light of the big bang. The moonlight reflected off her flawless surface, except the half moon her pussy made beneath her leather skirt.

She held a sign up: MISSED YOU LAST NIGHT.

She leaned hard against the railing of her balcony, as if she ached to be examined. She begged for his eyes to write their signature on her skin. He knew this was no striptease. This was a form of sacred dance.

"I am the witness to her light," he whispered back to her. He was sure she heard even at this distance. They took mutual comfort in anonymous distances. Sara shone with immunity and amusement. Her clothes were an unnecessary ornament before the face of the universe. Her nakedness was a form of religious pilgrimage, an act of ecclesiastical devotion.

He saw Sara in four dimensions, not three. Desire magnified the intensity of his seeing. Thomas saw star systems glow inside her skin. Her skin did not reflect the moon, it refined the curves of ancient seas, smoothed over with the naked absence of gravity and the silence of aching hands. Thomas's eye initiated his heart, and he perfected her body with the prayerfulness of his sight.

Thomas wanted to know more about Sara's man and if he saw her with the same depth and intensity that Thomas did. He wanted to know if her skin evoked in him mythic voyages and apocalyptic erections. Did his retinas burn with energy and ecstasy? Thomas wanted to know if he *cherished* her, or if her body just lay against his eyelid like a dead leaf.

Thomas hoped he was a dead man, a walking corpse, like so many he knew. That he could not see Sara as Thomas did. How could he? How could he see the galaxies glowing inside her?

"He has no eye," Thomas thought. "He has no vision in the retina of his heart."

5.

The next night, a slick film of cosmic dust and old stars surrounded Europa and Callisto. Sara was there again, leaning over her balcony. Her dreamy eyes and her refractable body reflected light at intimate angles. Light circled her thighs, and their eyes touched in a shared field of astrological vision.

She bent over the opposite railing with her pussy facing Thomas. Her musky breath almost fogged up his lens. He perfected her body with the prayerfulness of his sight.

He focused on the two hemispheres of her ass, round and smooth, twin moons hiding a shy sun. She placed her hands on each side of her ass and stretched out her pussy, her cunt a cluster of stars.

Sara was wet from his watching. She felt the specific gravity of his eye, and Thomas saw the shiny places on her lips. Her pussy was red and swollen, begging to be explored with probes and scopes and manned and unmanned extraterrestrial instruments. Constellations swirled around her cunt. Her pussy shone like Cassiopeia. He held her inside the warmth of his eye for a moment so intense it seemed like an eternity. She was slick as Callisto; he could see the shine on her thighs. She held up her sign:

TOMORROW NIGHT, 10.

DON'T MISS IT,

SARA

6.

He liked the precision of her invitation. At ten, he set the GPS and zero in the starfinder. He waited, swinging the telescope around the astrological houses. He caught the cooler, red stars of Aquarius and the hotter, white stars of Libra. He waited, and ten minutes later, the surface of her star-staggering body bent the light in his lens.

The sky was crammed with luminous spheres, but nothing compared to Sara's conspicuous body. Stars swelled in her skin. Her cunt was a spiral constellation, her body tattooed with stars and the magic of each of their names: Cygnus "the Northern Cross," and Vega and Altair, and Albireo "the Swan."

Thomas named all the stars rising inside her skin.

That night held an autumn moon, with a red hue descending. Sara's skin was washed in roses. Her nipples, already red and swollen, begged to be bitten. Sara fanned her nipples with the palm of her hand. Her hand trickled down her sides like light dripping out of a quasar.

Sara spread her legs and leaned into the balcony. Nothing interfered with their line of sight. Her cunt was a cool star, a radiant body waiting for its turn in paradise. They touched through the grace of their intuitive hearts.

Sara dipped one finger inside herself. She had tested the waters there many times, but each time was still a mystery. She went way up to the second knuckle. Sara eased it out, shiny and slick. She initiated another, then another until a forest of fingers clustered inside her. Thomas poured over her erotic piety like a monk over a sacred parchment.

Then, staring at Thomas, Sara licked her fingers, one by one, letting them linger in her mouth. Her fingers were like words she was waiting for, listening for, hoping for. Her fingers smelled like scrolls of some ancient spell, some taste of a handful of heaven. She savored herself the way astronomers envy stars.

She smiled the smile of the ever-blessed, and then left. Thomas was just about to step back from the eyepiece when Sara returned. This time, her sign said:

Surprise tomorrow.
Watch.

7.

That night, the man parted the curtain behind her like a confessional. He was flat-bellied, firm-chested, and long-limbed. He was so beautiful, Thomas couldn't be jealous. So graceful, he seemed to float behind her, like an asteroid orbiting the moon of her ass. She relished it. He saw her cunt swell like the tides of Mars, all curved and rising. Sara received her pleasure both ways, sandwiched between his touch and Thomas's sight.

She bent down in front of him as in some ancient rite evoked for the initiated and the innocent. She bent her head back and cupped his cock in her hands and tipped it up. Then she opened her mouth.

Thomas breathed in short, hungry bursts. His whole body pressed into the telescope, rocking it with the rhythms he was seeing. The man tossed his own head back and exhaled a fountain of stars, long strands of angels, wings and all. Sara opened her mouth and caught it all. Light swallowed light and the whole visible spectrum.

His breath reached out through the lens and brushed the insides of her thighs. He took her most intimate admissions from impersonal distances. He let his heart see. He didn't just look at her, he *beheld* her. He cherished her with his telescopic arousal. He came so close he could hear her cunt sigh. Space was no emptiness separating them—it was an umbilical cord connecting them. His eyes were the scouts of his heart. They tracked her every orbit, the exquisite azimuth of her eyelash, the trajectory of her flushed cheek

"Anyway," Thomas thought, "distance is an illusion promulgated by the short-sighted."

Sara mouthed words to Thomas, her lips round and red in the half-light.

"Let's start creation all over again," she said. "Let's lick light off each other until it hurts."

Her tongue ticked the words as she spoke and they came out smiling.

THE ASTRONOMER

Thomas had taught about the heavens his whole career. He opined about the theological dimensions of angels and analyzed the formulas of signs and wonders. He lectured on the glorious proportions of paradise and the truth of the expanding universe.

Yet there was no more palpable angel than Sara. She was the firmest prophecy of heaven. Thomas read the future in her telepathic skin. He licked stars from the curves of her body. She opened to him, and the sun fell from finite darkness into infinite light.

VISUAL MEMORY

Teresa Noelle Roberts

The memory came back to me again today in the studio, stepping between me and the canvas, slipping into what I was trying to paint and transforming it into something that didn't match my original vision. It's far better than the original vision—warmer and more sensual and more pleasing than the abstract color study of spring hills I'd had in mind—but it never fails to disarm me when I get derailed by the memory that way.

Especially when the results are as striking as they are this time, adding an erotic overtone to something that hadn't started out that way and that still, on the surface, doesn't seem like it should be sexual.

I imagine everyone has mental images they treasure and others that they'd love to forget but can't, that pop up at odd moments. I have my share of both. Some of mine, though, are oddly intense. Maybe it's because I always knew I wanted to paint and have spent my life consciously trying to commit images to memory, or maybe it happens to everyone, but most people don't talk about it. In any case, certain memories come back in hallucinatory detail, unravel time back to that moment and make me temporarily forget the present in the face of this vivid slice of the past.

Sunrise over the Atlantic on Midsummer Day. A castle emerging out of fog as we rounded a bend in the Welsh countryside. My grandmother, eighty years old and radiant, saying "I do" to the man she'd fallen in love with after twenty years alone. Two black horses, nose to nose, under a huge sycamore tree in a stone-walled pasture near an eighteenth-century farm in Connecticut.

And the first time I saw other people having sex.

That one doesn't have the obvious awesome beauty of sunrise softening crashing waves to pastel poetry, but it comes back often, and every time it does, it transforms me a bit, as it did when it happened. It's present tense, always, although it happened decades ago. An eternal now of the senses.

It's an unseasonably warm, late-April Saturday in 1983, and I'm sitting in my dorm room with the big windows wide open, having a beer and enjoying the rich smells of spring wafting in from the campus. The beer is Pabst Blue Ribbon, sharp and thin; even to my unsophisticated nineteen-year-old palate, it's dreadful, but it was on sale for something like two bucks a six-pack, and art students, the next best thing to beggars, can't be choosers. The smells, on the other hand, are fresh and wonderful: new grass and tree pollen and mud, almost enough to drown out the smells of paint and clove cigarettes that always linger in my room.

The young grass is the vivid green of my dad's goofiest golf pants; the sky is postcard caliber; and even the dull cinderblock gray of the squat 1960s dorms on the quad looks better than usual. I'm musing idly about that when something far more interesting catches my attention.

My dorm is *L*-shaped, and I'm on the inside of the *L,* which means there's a window catty-corner from mine. A whole wall of them, in fact, with their hideous orangey-red Venetian blinds more often than not drawn across their big, awkward picture windows.

But today the blinds of the room almost directly across from me are open.

And in the window I can see two naked people making out like there's no tomorrow. He's playing with her bountiful breasts, and I wish I had binoculars because from here it looks like she's got that special expression, the one I've felt on my own face but never seen on anyone else's, the smile you wear when you're not just crazy turned on, but also high on the power of your body over your guy's.

And while I feel like I should look away, like it's rude to watch this private moment, there's no power on earth to tear my eyes away from the spectacle.

I know the couple vaguely: Jenny, a tall, plump, quiet girl with long, brown hair who's either a history or anthro major, and Al, a bespectacled, nervously energetic guy (engineering? chemistry?) who looks more like a high school kid than a college junior. He'd be a cute high school boy—my kid sister would squeal over him— but for his age, he's on the small and scrawny side, especially contrasted with his silent giant of a girlfriend.

Not ugly people, but not what I'd normally call a hot couple, either.

But now everything's changed. With her fat-girl clothes shucked, Jenny looks strong and self-assured, like an Amazon or a plump but powerful Rubens nude. She has luscious curves where I'd have thought she only had bulges, and they're the kind of curves that I'd love to draw and that a guy would love to get his hands on and that I think I wouldn't mind getting my hands on, either, although such a thing hasn't occurred to me before.

Nudity hasn't transformed Al as magically as it has Jenny. He's still young looking, still geek-pale. Only, I can see hints of muscle that I hadn't imagined. Maybe *slender* would be a better word than *scrawny*. Still could use another twenty pounds on him, but what's there is proportioned nicely, and without his unfortunate glasses and with his own version of the beatific sex-smile, he's looking pretty damn good.

And when he turns a bit, bending to capture one of Jenny's fat nipples in his mouth, I make a strangled noise of surprise.

This skinny kid has the largest and most beautiful cock I've ever seen. Not that my sampling has been all that wide in real life, but it's been broad enough for me to realize that Jenny is a very lucky girl.

I start to settle down to enjoy the show. But first I grab my sketch pad. I'm into abstract art and political statements at this point in my life, and not much into life drawing—I figure if you want naturalism, that's what cameras are for—but the models in my mandatory life-drawing classes were never doing anything this interesting.

They're really getting into it now, and my frantic sketching can barely keep up. Jenny's got her hands on Al's big dick and is pumping away. I can catch glimpses of the purplish head, can imagine the slick precome that must be emerging to ease her hand along. I can't see what he's doing in return, but from the look on her face—eyes screwed shut, head thrown back, mouth moving as if she's moaning encouragement—he's got to be stroking between her legs and doing it well.

The play of line and shadow is beautiful, but it's hard to glance away long enough to do even the roughest of sketches. They're too fascinating, too delicious to watch.

When he falls to his knees and buries his face in the nest of pale brown hair between her legs, I can imagine the mingled smells of man and woman in heat—and it's easy to imagine the woman smell because I can feel it rising off me.

When Jenny starts to come, the pencil goes slack in my hand. Maybe the artistic skills of someone older and wiser and more talented could capture this, but I'm not up to the challenge. Even with her face distorted, or maybe because of it, she looks like a goddess. I swear, although maybe it's my imagination, that I can see her breasts flush, see the flush travel up and illuminate her face. I can certainly see her scream. She's loud enough that I can faintly hear it across the courtyard.

Her pleasure echoes through me. I clench, so close to coming from what I've seen that I can't resist brushing the pencil end against my clit, through my skirt. That's enough to spark an orgasm, not a full-blown screaming and shuddering production like Jenny's but a lighter one that sends waves of warmth throughout my whole body. For a second all I see are negative images, white against black and sparks of light against my screwed-up eyelids.

By the time I'm looking again, Al and Jenny have moved to the bed, and by the way they've positioned themselves—doggie style and kind of askew on the bed, so I see the penetration and still at least catch their faces in profile—I'm sure that, even if they'd started out with the blinds open from horny absentmindedness, they now know I'm watching and are getting off on it.

I've never seen myself being fucked. Almost all my sex has been in narrow dorm room beds, with no way to look in a mirror. I've glanced up or down to see the guy moving in me, his shaft getting slick and greasy-looking with my juices, and that was exciting. But I've never gotten the full effect until now of how two people look moving together.

I've never seen anything more beautiful—not just hot but

aesthetically stunning. His pallor looks like ivory next to her warmer peachy tones. The pendulous curve of her belly is no less beautiful than that of her breasts; the hips I'd call "chunky" and "bony" with clothes on look glorious as they snap together and apart. Her long hair's falling forward, obscuring her face, but even that makes a lovely line. His hair is sticking straight up like a punker's, and it brings out planes in his face I never would have imagined.

I can even see the muscles in her forearms twitching.

I'd always known the human body in motion could be beautiful. I'd never known how beautiful—or that the beauty was there in every body, waiting for the right circumstances to bring it out.

And I'd never known how horny I could get from a show like this, more turned on than I've ever been when I was actually fucking. Sex, to date, has been enjoyable but not earth-shattering. This looks like it's earth-shattering for Jenny and Al, and it's rubbing off on me. Juices are starting to ooze down my thighs, and I'm feeling needier in the face of Al's unreachable cock than I ever have been when one was handy.

I'm in one of my usual paint-stained long, black skirts (I have a rough dozen of them, in different stages of Death by Art), with no underwear because laundry day is tomorrow, after I get paid for my work-study job and I'll have the couple of bucks to do it. It's a simple matter to wriggle the skirt up and plunge into my own wetness. I'm so entranced by the show that I don't even worry that I'm giving one myself, to Al and Jenny (not that they seem to be paying attention to anything except each other) or anyone in the other wing who looks my way.

I'm torn, though. I want to draw them, capture them in their moment of peak passion. At the same time, I want to get off. Need to get off.

Art or orgasm? Tough call.

Then Al and Jenny make the decision for me. Al starts moving faster, pounding into her like a wild animal, and she bucks back against him as if trying to get all of his slim body inside her, not just his dick. This can't last long, and it's obvious that there's no time to make a decent sketch from life, so I start moving my hands to their furious rhythm. About the time the room shatters around me into colorful kaleidoscope-like patterns, they collapse onto the bed.

One of them, and I can't tell which, raises a lazy hand and closes the blind.

I still have the sketches I drew later that day in a frenzied trance of art and lust. They're good—not my best work by any means, or even my best work from my college days, but they have a raw erotic energy that makes them jump off the page.

It's a quality I strive for now in my art.

That afternoon marked a change in my work, although I didn't recognize it right away. I began to see the human body, and the whole natural world, in a different way. I looked at some of the older paintings I'd found boring and recognized the sensuality I'd seen between Jenny and Al blazing in an Ingres nude or smoldering below the surface of one of John Singer Sargent's respectable portraits of nineteenth-century Boston Brahmin ladies. I asked myself how much of my abstract and "political" artwork I did because it really was my style and how much was a way to play it safe, to keep my work from being too personal and emotionally charged. Too passionate.

And I began, cautiously at first, and then with more abandon, to incorporate more sensuality and passion into my work.

It wasn't an easy lesson, though. To this day, it's sometimes easier to hold back, to focus on form and color and line without emotional content, or to retreat to the easy realm of satire. When I realize that my work feels stale and cold, I call on the memory of Al and Jenny and invite their passion to help me.

And sometimes, like today, my subconscious catches me in an artistic cheat and they turn up unbidden—a mental movie reel that takes me back to a spring day in 1983 and brings its joyous sexuality to life in my mind and on my canvas.

A GIRL, TWO GUYS, AND A SEX TOY

Kristina Wright

New Year's Eve. Probably the most depressing holiday to be alone. It's even more depressing than Valentine's Day, because you can get away with saying you had to work on Valentine's Day and didn't have time for all the romantic stuff. But everyone knows when you're alone on New Year's Eve. They ask you who you kissed at midnight, and you have a choice of telling the truth and saying you were curled up in bed alone (which is depressing) or lying and saying you kissed some fabulous guy (which is depressing *and* pathetic).

I don't know why I always seem to end up alone on New Year's Eve, especially, in this case, when I actually had a boyfriend right up until Chrismukkah. I think David and I were just hanging on through the holidays, until he could figure out a way to break up with me without ruining my Hanukkah and until I could accept he was breaking up with me while acknowledging I would be paying for his Christmas presents well into the new year. Whatever the case, it was over. Dead. Finished. My menorah was tucked away, along with the trinkets and gifts David had gotten me (none of which were especially sentimental or romantic, so I felt disinclined to return them) and I was, once again, single.

Single girls don't have a lot of choices on New Year's Eve. Blind dates are out of the question; ditto, hanging with married or coupled friends. We singletons are left out in the cold on the romantic holidays, so I did what any tough, resilient girl should do—I invited all my like-minded, newly broken up or between relationships or simply single-by-choice friends to a little New Year's Eve party at my place.

If I was going to suffer, I decided, I would not suffer alone. There was plenty of bubbly in the fridge and music on the stereo, and I'd gotten my daily cry out of the way before anyone arrived. By ten o'clock, the music was cranked up loud enough to wake the neighbors, except most of them were in my apartment, and I found myself cuddled up in bed with two men.

Kevin and Michael were once my two best buddies. There was a lot of flirting and teasing, but I'd never slept with either of them. David was ridiculously jealous of my friendship with them, so I'd kind of distanced myself to keep the peace. I hadn't expected them to show and had felt a twinge of guilt for calling them at the last minute, but I guess they missed me as much as I missed them, because they showed up. I don't think I've ever been quite so happy to see two men as when I opened the door and Kevin thrust a magnum of champagne at me.

"So you didn't forget us, after all," Michael said, giving me a bear hug.

I laughed and hugged him back, then gave Kevin a squeeze. "I never forgot about you. I was just being stupid."

"Translation: You were in love." Kevin said "in love" with the same distaste I have when I say, "I have cramps."

I didn't want to dwell on my misery and, to be honest, laughing with my old friends made me forget just how miserable I thought I was. Somehow, we took our little party into my bedroom at some point. I didn't have any ulterior motive other than to get away from the noise. There was a rowdy game of strip poker going on in the living room and some drunken groping up against the refrigerator between two guys I thought were straight. As interesting as all that was, I found myself pulling Kevin and Michael into my bedroom and pushing them down on the bed.

"Damn, girl, you're strong," Michael said with a grin. "Should we strip down, or do you want to do the honors yourself?"

I laughed and flung myself on the bed between them, ignoring their half-hearted attempts to grab me. "Neither. I want to know what's been going on with you guys. I've *missed* you."

We spent the next hour lying on my bed, drinking champagne and catching up. I didn't even care that I was neglecting the rest of the gang; it felt too good to be cuddled up with my two favorite guys. I felt like I was reclaiming myself after a long, long time.

At some point while Kevin was regaling me with a story about his ski trip to Vermont, Michael started snooping through the stack of gift boxes next to my bed. I didn't think much about it as he looked at the boots my parents had gotten me and the scarf my sister Ruth had sent, until he pulled out the gag gift my best friend Kaitlin had given me, along with the note, "To help you get over David until the real thing comes along." The dildo looked ridiculous in Michael's hands—ridiculous and just as gigantic as I remember.

"What's this, your new boyfriend?" he asked

Kevin's eyes went wide, and I pounced on Michael to get the thing away from him. Between the champagne and wrestling with Michael (and somehow ending up sprawled on top of Kevin), I started to get horny. It hadn't been that long, really—only three weeks or so, though the last few times with David were lackluster at best (How do you know when a relationship is dead? When the sex is as much fun as doing the dishes). But now my hormones were raging, and I could tell I was soaking wet by the heavy, swollen feeling of my pussy.

All of this is an excuse for why, when Michael asked me if I'd played with my new toy, I didn't say, "No." I said, "Not yet." My voice sounded sultry and full of promise, even to me.

"Do you want to?" Kevin asked.

I snuggled back against the pillows, eyes closed. "Oh, yeah. Yeah, I do." And I did. I was so wet and hot, I could barely stand it. My body was throbbing in time to the bass of the stereo. I couldn't make out the song, but the thump-thump-thump of the bass made the walls—and my skin—vibrate. My clit quivered to be touched and stroked in time to that thumping bass and, looking from Michael to Kevin, I decided I didn't want them to do it. I wanted to do it while they watched.

"What are you going to do, babe?" Michael's voice was low and pure sex. There was no mistaking his erection, and though I'd known him for years, I blushed.

I blushed, but it didn't stop me from shimmying out of my jeans and panties. I sat there between two of my oldest, platonic male friends, naked except for a thin tank top that did more to accentuate my hard nipples than hide them, and spread my legs.

I could practically feel the heat of their gaze between my legs. Instead of clamping my thighs together, I spread wider, throwing a leg over each of them. "Give me that thing."

Michael wasted no time in handing me that gigantic dildo, his expression one of lustful anticipation.

I swallowed hard as I hefted the weight of the dildo in my hand. It was even bigger than I remembered. When I had opened it, I had told Kaitlin there was no way that thing was getting anywhere near my tender bits. Now, with a deep breath, I pressed the head between the wet, wet lips of my pussy. I took another deep breath. I couldn't do this, could I? I couldn't fuck myself with this monster in front of two of my friends. I wasn't sure which bothered me more—the size or the fact that Kevin and Michael were watching me, but I started to chicken out.

"This isn't going to work," I muttered, more to myself than them. "I can't do this."

Michael leaned down and whispered in my ear, "You're so fucking sexy."

Kevin one-upped him by putting his hand on mine and giving the dildo a little nudge toward my pussy. "You know you want it. Do it for us. Fuck yourself."

I was dripping wet, and my head was spinning from too much champagne and the relief that comes after a bad break-up and the prospect of starting the new year with a clean slate and having two friends, two amazing friends, in bed with me. Oh, who am I kidding? All those things may be true, but what made me go through with it was the fact that I was feeling as slutty as a cat in heat and all I wanted to do was get fucked. *Now.*

With Kevin's hand over mine, I pushed the dildo inside my wet cunt. Slowly. Really, really slowly. All three of us gasped when the head made an audible, wet pop as it went inside me. It was one of the sexiest, raunchiest moments of my life to look down between my legs and see two men staring at my cunt being stretched open by a huge dildo.

I whimpered. My thighs trembled. With Kevin helping me, I eased the dildo into my engorged cunt. If I hadn't been so damned wet, it might have hurt to be stretched by something nearly as big as my fist. Instead, I only wanted more.

Michael kissed me. "Good girl," he said. I remember him saying that over and over again. "Good girl, good girl."

For some reason, his words soothed me and made me even hotter at the same time. I wanted to please them. I wanted to fuck myself for them. I lay there with my eyes closed, knowing they were watching me, knowing they could see everything. They could see *me* like no one has ever seen me before. Sure, I'd played around with sex toys before and even brought them to bed on occasion for an interesting threesome, but the lights were always dim when there was a guy in bed with me, and there was other stuff going on at the same time. Now I felt like I was center stage, the star of the show, and judging by the appreciative comments and heavy breathing, the audience loved the performance.

When I looked down again, I had taken over half the dildo inside me. I felt so stretched and full I could barely breathe. I could hear the party going on just beyond my bedroom door, and a small voice in the back of my brain asked whether I had remembered to lock the door. The truth was I was too far gone to care. I looked down at Michael and Kevin, so close to the action they had to be able to smell me as well as see every detail, and all I cared about was getting off. Hard.

Kevin leaned down, presumably to get a closer look, and I could feel his breath on my clit. I moaned from the sensation and lifted my hips. I couldn't bring myself to ask for what I needed, but he must have known because he licked my clit. It was quick, no more than a mere brush of his soft, wet tongue against my engorged, wet clit, but a jolt of arousal so strong I cried out went through me. He licked my clit to the same rhythm I fucked myself to with that enormous cock while Michael fondled my breasts and tweaked my nipples through my tank top. The combination of sensations was overwhelming. I rocked my hips forward to take the dildo into me and felt Kevin suck my clit between his lips. Every time I rocked forward, he sucked. I rocked and he sucked until every fiber of my being strained to come. It was right there, just beyond my grasp. Then Kevin sucked my clit and Michael rolled my nipples between his fingers and I rocked on that thick dildo in my cunt in just the right combination that I came. I came and came and came, like I had never come before.

I came so hard and so long, I thought I was going to pass out. I was oblivious to everything except the sensations coursing through my body. I was pressed between Michael and Kevin, their warm, clothed bodies feeling so incredibly good against my sensitive skin. I didn't know when they had moved up the bed, I just knew I never wanted them to leave. I wanted to stay like that, nestled between them, forever.

Kevin was the first to break the silence. "Wow."

I giggled, and then winced, as I slid the dildo out of my still throbbing pussy. "Um...thanks?"

"No kidding, wow," Michael said, sounding as dazed as I felt. "That was fucking incredible."

"Happy New Year, kid." Kevin kissed my forehead. "I'm going to have a hard-on until June, but I wouldn't have missed this for anything."

I couldn't stop giggling. I squirmed and twisted between them like a playful puppy, conscious of their erections but equally conscious of the fact neither was asking for more. There were knocks at the door and people wishing us happy New Year, and I realized that at some point during my personal festivities, I had missed midnight. I didn't care. This was better than any ball dropping.

I didn't fuck Kevin and Michael that night. What I had shared with them couldn't be improved upon, as far as I was concerned. Judging by their contented expressions when the three of us settled down to sleep that night, they agreed with me.

At least, until the next morning...

OPERATIC ECSTASY

Erica DeQuaya

Edward grimaced and shifted in his seat for what seemed like the hundredth time. Attending the opera hadn't been his idea of a number one great time when Genera had brought it up earlier. But he'd relented and he was here. Problem was, sitting next to his elegantly dressed wife was bringing something else up. And given Genera's rapt attention to *The Magic Flute,* Edward didn't think now was the time to let her know he was interested in nothing more than ripping off her clothes and having his way with her.

Shifting yet again, hoping to ease the pressure on his throbbing groin, Edward wondered why he'd agreed to this evening out.

"You write plays for a living, and I act in them. I'm trying to direct one, and you want to *see* a play tonight?" he'd snapped at Genera earlier. He hadn't meant to be so snippy. But she'd reached him during a break smack in the middle of tech week.

Edward hated tech week.

Tech week was when rehearsals sucked, actors were cantankerous, and techies became even more impatient than usual. As a theater actor, he was used to it. But his role was different this time. He was the director, trying to pull together Clifford Odet's play *Awake and Sing* for an opening in two weeks. He had his hands full trying to mold his prima donna actors into a Depression-era Jewish family. But nothing was falling together, and if it collapsed on opening night, as he feared it would, there'd be no doubt as to who would shoulder it all.

He could almost see the smirking headlines in newspaper art sections across Manhattan and the five boroughs: "Award-Winning Actor Flops in Directorial Debut."

With all that weighing on his mind, the last place Edward had wanted to be was in another theater house, watching another performance. All he'd wanted to do was go home, belt back a scotch, sink into a hot tub, then go to bed.

But Genera'd had other ideas.

"It's not a play," she'd responded calmly to his irritation. "It's an opera. A *Mozart* opera."

Of course. Like the composer would really make a difference.

"I'm exhausted," he'd told her. "The last thing I want to do is see another staged production—"

But Genera had been insistent. "A night out will do us both good."

Edward had given up arguing with her, figuring putting on a suit and tie and taking her to dinner and *The Magic Flute* was less a hassle than fighting. Three years into his marriage with her, Edward adored his wife. But he was realistic, too. Genera could be as flexible as a brick wall when her mind was made up about something.

Besides, she'd been right about one thing. It had been a while since they'd gotten dressed up and gone to see something that neither of them had written, directed, or acted in. By the time Edward had met Genera at a small restaurant at the Upper West

Side, he'd been okay, even looking forward to the evening. He was even more grateful to find the nearby theater only half full. Edward didn't like crowds.

The production was exquisite. After a while, Edward found himself enjoying the opera, becoming involved in the touching love story between the hero and the heroine—Tamino and Tamina—admiring them for their willingness to brave everything—even the wrath of the Queen of the Night—to be together.

But it all began to fall apart as Genera's perfume danced around his senses, wrapping him in a sensual allure that left him almost breathless. Swallowing, Edward glanced at her. She'd gone all out in the dress-up department tonight, wearing a black velvet number that stopped at mid-thigh and showed a nice amount of cleavage. Different from her usual outfit of jeans, workshirts, and overalls. There were days Edward forgot Genera had legs or breasts, the way she kept them covered up outside the bedroom.

Not tonight, though. Tonight, both were gloriously on display. And it was making him damned uncomfortable.

Despite his almost painful arousal, Edward smiled to himself at the rapt look on Genera's face, illuminated by the soft light from the stage. His wife had a street rep as being overly aggressive with her productions, a writer who brooked no nonsense from actors or directors. She could get away with the bitch playwright act, too, as everything she wrote was gold, and most of the theater community in New York and elsewhere knew it. But Edward knew Genera was a softie when it came to romance. *The Magic Flute* fit her idealistic views on relationships perfectly.

Right now, though, Edwards thoughts were on the seamier side of romance. The dirty, raunchy side. Hot and fast sex—as much and as often as possible. Genera's slick, wet walls contracting around his rock-hard penis, almost to the point of agony. The taste of her cream as he tongued between her legs, hearing her ecstatic screams while he drove her to a hard, violent orgasm. The musk of her arousal assaulting him, drugging him, driving him into a sensual frenzy. Genera had a way of gasping at the back of her throat when she was close to coming. As he sat among the music and duets and chaste romantic dance between two young lovers onstage, Edward suddenly wanted to hear that gasp. Badly.

He shifted uncomfortably yet again, cursing as his cock rubbed against his briefs. He ached to touch her but was reluctant to disturb her absorption in the opera. With an inward sigh, he settled for sliding his hand behind her neck and fondling the soft, short hair there. It wasn't doing much for his hard-on, but at least it was something. Hopefully, it wouldn't disrupt her too much.

But as his fingers glided along the back of her neck and through her silky hair, he felt her shiver. She was still for a moment. Then, keeping her eyes on the stage, she took his hand from her neck and brought it to her mouth. Edward's breath caught as Genera slowly kissed his fingers, her warm lips caressing each one. Her lips moved slowly over his palm, her tongue reaching out and flicking insolently against the sensitive flesh, again and again. The wetness fueled his lust, and Edward barely restrained himself from groaning.

Her attention still apparently on the opera, Genera slowly moved his hand from her lips and slid it provocatively over her body, over the exposed flesh of her chest and the upper part of her breasts, across the soft black velvet, then under the hem of her dress. Edward sat still, gritting his teeth, feeling hot lust pound through his veins as she urged him gently up her thigh. She wore stockings and a garter belt, rather than typical pantyhose, and he didn't resist as she pushed his hand past the silken hose, to the bare, warm flesh of her upper thigh and beyond. He stopped suddenly and swallowed in disbelief.

Genera wasn't wearing any underwear.

She turned to him, a slight smile touching her lips. She moved her mouth, and he saw the words forming in the dim light:

Do me. Now.

She spread her legs slightly and leaned back, closing her eyes. Edward sat for a long moment, stunned, only dimly aware of the operatic gymnastics continuing onstage. He looked at Genera, her sexy dress rucked high on her thighs, legs spread in a wanton offering, her body screaming its invitation for his touch. He wondered where all of this was coming from. Not that he was complaining. But this wasn't like her. Genera wasn't into public displays of affection; she hated even holding hands in public. Just the other day, he'd had teased Genera about her reluctance to kiss or touch him in public. As a joke, he'd dared her to try to seduce him in public.

She was now apparently taking him up on that dare. He realized, suddenly, what this evening was all about and, despite his sexual excitement, had to restrain a laugh.

Be careful what you wish for.

Breath raw in his throat, Edward moved his fingers between her legs, stroking the fine, soft hair, feeling her moist warmth. His cock twitched and he closed his eyes. Genera's brazenness, her aggression, her demand to be serviced in the middle of this opera, with elegantly dressed people surrounding them, was a huge turn-on.

Opening his eyes, Edward pushed deeply between her nether lips, stroking the slick folds of her arousal, hearing her soft moans. Even through the blood lust roaring through his ears, he heard Tamino and Tamina sing of their love for one another, and reflected that he'd never feel the same way about Mozart or *The*

Magic Flute again. He wouldn't be able to hear this particular duet without seeing his wife's flushed face and submissive stance in his mind's eye. He wouldn't be able to think about Tamino or Tamina without the memory of Genera's juicy pussy under his seeking fingers.

Edward touched her hard, swollen clit, and Genera caught her breath, spreading her legs wider to give him easier access. His fingers slid into her, her juices providing easy entry. He found the roughness of her G-spot and pressed hard in the way he knew she liked. About ready to lose control himself, Edward waited until he sensed her close to the edge, then withdrew his fingers to fondle her swollen folds. Genera opened her eyes, her lips forming an almost soundless plea. She squirmed in her chair, her body clearly demanding its release, but Edward stroked her outer lips almost tenderly, cooling her excitement until the next go-round.

Trembling, in the throes of his own incredible lust, Edward pushed his fingers deeply into her soaked and engorged pussy again, hearing her give a soft, abbreviated moan. He suddenly itched to make her come; he wanted to make her lose control. They'd probably be thrown out if they were spotted. But right now, he didn't give a damn. All he wanted was to give his lady the ultimate pleasure of a forbidden and very public orgasm.

Fingers trapped by her tight, wet hole, Edward massaged her clitoris hard with this thumb, demanding her climax. Genera's eyes flew open. She writhed desperately in her seat in silent, ecstatic excitement as he continued his intimate, demanding caresses.

But Edward was near his own breaking point. As he sensed her coming down, he abruptly stood, took her hand, and practically dragged her from the seat. Genera followed his lead without protest, and they left the theater. White-hot desire pounding through his veins, urgency driving him, Edward sought out someplace relatively hidden, where they could have a modicum of privacy. That was difficult in this particular venue, but he was heartened to see the lobby was almost empty. Hesitating only for a moment, Edward urged her to a darkened hallway in the area near the restrooms. Edward didn't care that they were separated from the opera-going public by only one thin wall. His hunger for her made such things irrelevant, and he pulled her against him roughly, capturing her lips with his, thrusting his tongue into her mouth and feeling it tangle with hers in wild abandonment. Potent lust surged through his body, and he backed her against the wall and brutally moved his hips against hers, dry-fucking her, his penis seeking her hot, wet core through their clothes. The scent of her perfume mixed with the overpowering musk of her arousal as she matched her hips to his movements.

Keeping her captive, Edward dipped his head, running kisses along her neck and then lower, his lips and tongue caressing the tops of her breasts. He was drugged with the feel and taste of her as she clung to him, trembling hard, her breath coming in gasps. Wanting more, Edward scooped his hands into her low-cut dress and freed one of her breasts, its ripe, rosy nipple begging to be licked and sucked. He slipped the taut peak into his mouth, hearing her moans as he nibbled gently, then almost savagely tongued the hardened flesh, his dick throbbing in agonized counterpoint to his actions.

As he worked on her nipple, Edward slid his hand beneath her dress, his palm moving against her rear end, fingers dipping into her crack.

"Eddie, please—"

Genera's voice was high, tense; Edward stopped teasing her nipple to look at her flushed face and tousled dark hair. Her eyes caught his, and in their light-gray depths Edward saw an insane, intense desire that matched his own.

"Take me, Edward. Please."

She gasped out her plea, and in response, Edward ruthlessly pressed his fingers against her crotch, delighting in her moans.

"Beg me again," he said hoarsely. "Do it, Gen."

"Please. Oh, God. Please. Do me."

She moved hard against his fingers, and Edward kissed her with a brutal passion. He broke the kiss, his own breath coming in rough gasps as he continued to finger her hot, wet core, bringing her close, then pulling back and grinning at her frustration.

"Beg me," he whispered harshly. "I want to hear you beg me again. But do it the way I like."

"Edward, damn you—"

"Beg me, or else I'll stop this right now."

"You're a bastard."

Smiling at her and using every ounce of his willpower, Edward removed his hand, and she swore at him.

"What do you want me to do to you?" he asked, almost gently. Though he felt ready to explode, he wanted to draw this out for as long as they could both stand it.

Genera rolled her head back against the wall, a picture of frustrated, agonized lust. "I can't. Oh, God, don't make me say it."

"Tell me." It was a game they played in bed, one they both enjoyed. He would force her to talk dirty to him, would make her scream the sex words at him before he granted her release. It was one way he enjoyed exerting control over his headstrong wife, and she willingly followed his lead, first pretending reluctance, than acceding to his wishes in ecstatic compliance.

Now Edward wanted to hear those dirty words drop from her lovely lips in public, where almost anyone walking by on the other side could hear. The thought of it brought him close to the breaking point, and he pressed his body against her, hard.

"Tell me," he hissed. "Tell me what you want me to do to you. Now, Gen."

"Edward... Oh, my God..."

"Tell me."

Yanking up the hem of her dress, Edward moved his clothed lower body against her nakedness, rubbing insistently against her soft belly. She bucked against him with a groan, her eyes glazed with excitement and need. He almost groaned himself, seeing her so wild, so uninhibited, so responsive to his words and touch.

"Tell me, Genera." He barely got out the words, his hunger for her tightening his throat.

Her restraint finally broke and she babbled her need, not caring that anyone might be listening. "I want you to fuck me. To put that hard cock of yours in me. To move inside me...hard, Edward. So hard. Oh, God...now...*please...*"

She grabbed at his arms, the almost desperate plea dropping from her lips. Impatient for her, Edward stepped away for a moment and unzipped his pants, awkwardly pulling them down with his briefs. He returned to her and in two swift movements, moved up and into her, burying his cock deeply in her soaking cunt, hearing her gasp as his balls tightened against her bottom.

Keeping her captive against the wall with his body and arms, Edward thrust against her, her slick, swollen walls providing an unbearable torture on his hardness, the white-hot throbbing between his legs shooting into his lower belly. Genera wriggled and he groaned, her motions sending fire through his veins, a heady desire begging to be quenched. He savaged her mouth again, wanting to taste her sweetness as his body rose toward an almost violent release. Then he was out of control, coming hard, crying out into her open, willing mouth. He tasted her moans as she followed suit, her orgasm ricocheting through her and communicating to him. Still hard inside her, feeling her vaginal muscles clench around him as she came violently, Edward felt heat swamp his body and he climaxed again.

In the aftermath, Genera almost collapsed against him, and Edward, trembling hard, held her close as he fought to breathe normally again. Reality teased his consciousness as he heard ushers pass by on the other side in preparation for opening the doors. In a moment, this area would be full of opera-going patrons taking a last-minute insurance run before heading home.

He shook his head and chuckled, sliding out of her and pulling up his underwear and pants. He met her amused and sated glance with his own smile.

"Lady, when you meet a challenge, you go all the way," he murmured.

"Isn't this what you were talking about the other day? About public displays of affection?"

He burst out laughing at her innocently phrased question. "I was talking about holding hands in public, Gen. Maybe exchanging a kiss or two."

"I'm sorry." She looked and sounded anything but as she smoothed her dress down around her legs and tucked her breast back into the neckline. "I guess I misunderstood."

He dropped a kiss on her temple, her cheek, enjoying the feel of her soft skin against his lips. "Looks like we missed the end of the show. I'm sorry, love."

"I think we had our own show," Genera said softly. "Edward, let's go home. Maybe we can make it in time for our own encore."

Insides quaking at her invitation, Edward smiled and offered his arm, and they left as the crowd began exiting the theater.

BEHIND THE WHEEL

L. Elise Bland

"Give me the keys," I told my husband. "I'm in the mood to drive." The shiny red pickup truck was officially mine, but somehow he always seemed to take the driver's seat. Reluctantly, he handed over the jangling ring of keys, and we set out to do our usual Tuesday-night grocery shopping, but with me behind the wheel. Riding with me is always an adventure, and this trip would prove even more memorable. As soon as we hit the road, I was taking one of my infamous "shortcuts," the kind that usually gets me lost and sends my husband into a frenzy.

"I told you to let me drive," he said, agitated. "You're going the wrong way again."

"No, I'm not," I said. "I have a surprise for you." I pulled down a secluded street and parked in a spot with just enough shadow and light to see and not be seen. I leaned over to the passenger's seat and unbuttoned his shirt. His chest is completely smooth except for a couple of sprouts of hair right between his pecs. He has the kind of torso that makes him forever young and that I never grow tired of kissing. I took a tiny man nipple into my mouth and lingered, listening to his heart race. He sounded as nervous as I felt. Slowly but surely, I made my way down his stomach only to find his cock already out of his pants and ready to go. So much for my surprise. He knows me all too well.

Unfortunately, married life had become somewhat predictable. But fortunately, I had recently learned some new tricks. According to many sex manuals, men are visual creatures. "When performing oral sex," one author suggests, "always make eye contact. Imagine yourself a porn actress." I had seen a few porn films in my life, so I had an idea of what a fancy blow job was supposed to look like, even though it was difficult to coordinate hands, mouth, and facial expressions, all while leaning over sideways in the front seat of a truck. Determined to be the dutiful wife, I flipped my hair back just so, making sure to keep it off his stomach to give him a clear view of all my tongue work. I took him in my mouth and played the starving vixen. I tried out every oral-fixation trick in the book, literally. I nibbled his cock like a corncob, licked it like an ice cream cone, sucked it like a lollipop, and sipped droplets from his head like honeysuckle syrup. I even added in a slurp and a cherry pop for special sound effects. He was in heaven, moaning and writhing in the passenger seat.

Just as I had feared and hoped, my show was interrupted by the low growl of an approaching vehicle. *Who could it be?* I wondered. *What if they see us? What if they don't see us?* When the car turned the corner, a sudden flash of silver headlights illuminated my husband's white physique, transforming him briefly into a rock-hard marble god. His cock stiffened in my mouth out of fear, and the intruder drove on, none the wiser. The scene was perfect. My "public blow job" plan was already paying off. He was hard, I was wet, and the adrenaline was flowing. And, I'll admit, I was doing a phenomenal job of sucking dick.

Then the unthinkable happened. In the midst of all the excitement, all the fanfare, and all the danger—with his cock buried deep in my throat, ready to explode any second—he yawned.

"Sorry," he said, covering his mouth. "Long day at work." He slipped his fingers into my hair in hopes of reclaiming the moment, but by that time, my mood had flown out the window. I sat up, face smeared with cock juice, and kicked the gas pedal in anger. My tough little red truck tore into the night, causing my husband to hold on for dear life. His still-wet cock bounced steadily along the bumpy road until I finally slammed on the brakes.

"Get out," I said flatly.

"What?" he asked. "Are you crazy?"

"I said *out*. O-u-t. This is my truck," I announced, as if he didn't know. "If you want to sit here and fight with me, then stay in the truck. Otherwise, get out." After five years of marriage, he knew when to obey. Eager to leave me alone, he opened the door and scrambled for his belongings, but only made it out with one flip-flop and his shorts.

"Call me when you wake up, sleepyhead," I yelled, throwing the cell phone out the window. *This will teach him a lesson*, I thought. I left him there, standing under the streetlight like a horny hustler. His abandoned cock formed a tent in his pants and cast a long, enticing shadow on the sidewalk, hoping and waiting for my hasty return. One lap around the block and all would be forgiven, and even more exciting the second time around.

I'll admit, I'm not the best driver in the world and tend not to bother with maps, but I do know the basics. A block is a block is a block, right? A big circle with edges. I took a turn at the next stop sign and drove down the street, careful not to go too fast. After all, the point was to scare him a little bit, and I didn't want the game to be over just yet. Two more right turns and I'd be back to pick up my honey, or so I thought. But before

I made it to the end of the street, I found myself in a cul-de-sac, a little turn-around that spat me right into another circle. Around the next corner, I delved deeper into the fuzzy world of ranch houses and twisted oaks. Corner after corner, and my husband was nowhere to be seen. Meaningless street signs whizzed by my window. Every empty, husbandless streetlight looked the same, and every yard of the sprawling neighborhood, identical. The night was dark and quiet, except for the faraway bark of a restless dog. Or maybe that was my husband.

Where was he? Where was that streetlight? I gripped the wheel in panic. I had every intention of exposing him, but never imagined my joke would last over five minutes. There was no denying it. I was lost. The game was over. I finally gave up and dialed his cell.

"Baby," I squeaked into the phone sheepishly. "I don't know where you are."

"Where the hell are you?" he yelled.

"Well," I stammered. "I hate to tell you this, but I don't know where I am, either."

"I'm at the corner of Greentree and Spicewood. I'm waving at you right now."

"That's not me," I said.

Another car passed by him. "Do you see me yet?" he asked, nervously. No, I didn't but apparently somebody else did. I heard a honk come through my cell phone. I was starting to worry that our kinky escapade was going to end up in the police station.

"I'm still on the main road—I think." I didn't know if I was going north, south, east, or west. But as panicked as I was, I was still enjoying the idea of my half-naked man standing out on the road with a hard-on, like a hot and desperate hitchhiker waiting just for me, if only I could get to him.

After much more meandering, I finally spotted his streetlight in the distance. There he was, pacing around shirtless and half shoeless, his phone glued to his ear. We were safe at last, but not for long.

Instead of rushing to his rescue, I had a devilish new idea. I stopped in front of a house half a block up the hill and killed the engine. No, my sexy truck adventure wouldn't be over so soon. I was still horny and I had my prey exactly where I wanted him. He had no choice but to play along. He was so cute, so anxious, still blurting meaningless directions into my ear: "Get on Greystone and take a left. Then take the second right..."

I had other things on my mind. I eased my seat back, propped my legs up on the dash, and let my mind wander into my panties. I was still soaking wet from sucking his cock earlier and charged up from being angry and lost.

"Are you still hard?" I asked him over the phone, opening my lips with two fingers. My pussy was begging to be filled, and he was so close and so good. On the one hand, I wanted to rescue him and fuck him right there in the back of the truck—after all, it's called a "truck bed" for a reason. But that would have been too predictable.

"No, not really too hard," he answered.

"Well, why would I want to come back for you if you aren't hard? Do something about it."

Silence.

"I'm not kidding. I'm going to quit looking for you if you don't get it back up." I watched him from the distance, one hesitant hand digging into his pocket in a feeble attempt to masturbate.

"Get that hand out of your pocket and do it right."

"Hey, wait. How did you know where my hand was?" Busted. He had found me out. "Where are you?" he asked, turning around in circles. "Come get me!"

"No, not until you're hard again. Come on. Pull it out for me." He held up his hand and shot his middle finger into the darkness. "I'm not kidding," I told him. "Whip it out, or else I leave." He looked to the left and then to the right. No cars were in sight, not even mine. As instructed, he unzipped his shorts and a bit of pink flesh emerged, the same flesh that I had so eagerly sucked earlier. When his strokes started up, I followed suit, keeping his rhythm that I already knew so well. With my thumb on my clit and my fingers deep inside, I watched his cock grow harder and harder, imagining with every beat that he was slamming me, winding me up, tightening me, screwing me, and truly fucking me, just a little pissed off at me—and maybe even a little scared of me.

"Come on baby, yank it for me," I said. "I've got your balls in my mouth. Jerk off on my face right now and I'll eat your cum. You know I love it." I dug my hand into my pussy and spouted out more smut. He didn't care what I said as long as it was nasty.

"I'm on my back. Sit on me. Fuck my tits, my big, soft tits pressed around your hard dick. Give me that pearl necklace I've always wanted, hot white drops all over my neck." I watched him intently. He was almost there and so was I.

"Now I'm right in front of you, bent over, my pussy and ass spread wide open. Sneak up behind me. Jerk off all over my pink crack. Make me hot and wet, dripping with cum." In his mind and his hand, he did everything I said, listening to my voice, pointing with his cock, and peering into the darkness to find his target. Then he leaned back and shot off, right there on the sidewalk, like some kind of wild nocturnal animal that had accidentally wandered into suburbia.

I braced my legs around the steering wheel, gave myself one last thrust, and came so hard my thigh tapped the horn.

Suddenly a porch light switched on. Without missing a beat, I cranked up the truck and rolled down the hill to retrieve my man. But instead of picking him up, I put the truck in park and crawled into the passenger seat.

"It's your turn to drive now," I said. And off into the darkness we sped.

SHE GRINDS HER OWN COFFEE

Cheri Magid

Duchamp here shows two different worlds separated by a metal bar and stuck between two large panes of glass. There is the feminine one above, the masculine down below. The bride, more an "it" than a person with her body like an amoeba and her machine-like arm, reaches towards the bachelors' realm. They however cannot reciprocate as they are locked in place, stuck behind a primitive contraption that to the eye—

Damn it. Would it kill Josie Pixler to use the spelling checker? She underlined the offending word in red ballpoint. Twice. "Use spell check!" Exclamation point. Exclamation point. Exclamation point.

She thought of Josie in the back corner of her History of Modern Art section slouching against the window. Josie with her dyed red hair, vintage gold heels, milky white skin, and look of perpetual boredom—a girl who thought she had nothing. She for one didn't buy it. As her TA, she could sense the fire, the intellect, that raged underneath. There were flashes of it in her papers. Why couldn't she get to her? There had been conferences. Tear-filled excuses as to why Josie kept cutting class. But try as she might, she could never reach bottom with her. She suspected that the disconnection was one of her own making. Had she been too hard on her?

"Bride Stripped Bare by Her Bachelors Even" then becomes a metaphor then for unmet desire. The question the artist poses then is, are we looking at a love machine or a thing of suffring? Rather than having her entreties met by the cowed bachelors, the bride is left alone to masturbate. Duchamp puts it this way: *"She grinds her own chocolate."*

What?! That part was dead wrong. It was the bachelors in the bottom panel who were "grinding their own chocolate." For God's sake, they were the ones standing by the chocolate grinder, which wasn't even in the same panel as the bride. How could she "grind her own chocolate" without a grinder?

She knew better, Josie did. They had discussed Duchamp's mythic views on women in class, the woman as consummator, as manipulator. She thought she could just spit back the gist of the piece and get away with it. It was a dare even if it was a lazy one.

She bit the end of the pen, chewed it up and down. Damn. There were five more papers to go through after Josie's. Each one would take at least a half an hour, which meant she wouldn't get to the gallery in East Williamsburg until at least six. By that time, Fernando would be gone, and she would have to hang the rest of the show herself.

She regretted taking the gallery job. True, it would look good on her résumé that she had started curating even before she had her master's. But the extra work meant yet another night without her beloved thesis. She missed Sophie like a dear friend who had all but disappeared on her. Sophie Calle, the sneaking art world wild woman of bravado and mischievousness. Sophie who in *Suite Vénitienne* disguised herself in a blond wig and glasses, followed a man she didn't know from Paris to Venice, and documented all his movements as she went. Sophie who in *The Sleepers* invited strangers to lie in her bed, then photographed them while they slept. If she closed her eyes and thought about it hard enough, she could see the whole of her bibliography piled haphazardly on the broken chair that served as her nightstand. All beckoning. All uncracked.

She looked down at her lackluster salad. She should eat it, anyway. As it was, she barely had enough cash to eat out these days. The gallery was supposed to contribute a rich eighty dollars for her troubles, but she doubted whether the check would clear. She knew she ought to start grading papers from home again. The thought of her hermetic studio with its dust bunnies, the dishes in the sink, the need at every corner, though, was too much. Why hadn't she ordered gnocchi like she had wanted to, something filling? Why did Italian restaurants think they should offer Greek salads, anyway?

Silvio must have sensed her frustration. He approached her suddenly. "Miss, you are not eating."

"Sorry. I am thinking." She tapped her temple for emphasis. Truthfully, she probably came to Gioia Mia to speak Italian. "You may take it, thank you. And may I have a coffee, Silvio? Thank you."

Actually, she knew why she came. Silvio's daughter wasn't much of a cook. But the espresso—that was another thing entirely. Rich, deep, syrupy—so sweet there'd be no need for sugar. A thick layer of khaki crema would line the cup, the spoon, her mouth with a luscious velvety froth. That initial tang of bitterness. That sweet wave of intensity which would follow. The insides of her cheeks tingled in expectation.

When it arrived, steaming and heady, she marveled at its simplicity and its decadence. The small, white ceramic cups. The delicate saucer. The spoon with the tiny slit of lemon rind. She raised it to her lips.

Across the café, a dark-haired man in a crisp white shirt was poised in the very same position. His mouth stopped in an aborted O, the cup barely skimming his parted bottom lip. There were five full seconds in which they were perfect mirrors of each other. Then they smiled, broke position.

"May you live a hundred years," she said after a moment, raising the cup in his direction.

"No English," he replied.

"Not English. Italian."

"No English."

His voice was smoky, a life of unfiltered cigarettes. Turkish? she wondered. She looked up, and their eyes met again. Black pools, as black as espresso. He held the tiny cup with a hand that was almost too large to contain it.

She drank in the rich shot of warmth. Now it was her fingers that were tingling. She closed her eyes, savored it, swallowed again. It was coating her insides with waves of the deepest chocolate.

Chocolate. She grabbed the pen. "Chips," she wrote on her hand. She had almost forgotten that she offered to make princess brownies for the opening. Did she have enough cream cheese at home? She dreaded opening the container to check, since whatever was in there was most likely green.

She heard the clink of ceramic on her table and looked up. Silvio was bringing her another espresso.

"Oh. No, I didn't—"

"The gentleman."

She glanced across the café. He was holding his cup in the same gesture as before, this time with the hint of a smile on his face. "*Sahtein,*" he said looking directly at her. Arabic? Her eyes took in his deep olive skin, the hint of shadow. A man who had to shave every morning. He would use a straight razor, she thought, a brush with a handle made of something fine, like tusk. His curly hair was meticulously pulled back at his nape, then discreetly tucked under. How far would it tumble down his neck if he were to loosen it?

The smell led her back to the coffee. She breathed it in. It intoxicated her, beckoned.

She knew better. She shouldn't have more than one cup. Her body tended to reject even the first, the initial sweetness and warmth always giving way to a rush of acid a few hours later. She should drink more water, instead. It would dilute the ill effects. Yes. But there it was at her elbow, anyway. So tiny. So perfect. And to refuse him. How would she go about explaining?

"*Sahtein,*" she repeated tentatively. She drew the cup to her lips, drank deeply, feeling the creaminess and the heat of it. A second passed, then quickened. She felt the rush of personality. The crawl of skin. The brightness of life. The shapes of shadows and buildings rendered solid. And the itch...

She didn't know why people went to bars to meet others of the opposite sex. Alcohol made her relax, of course, but it also rendered her sleepy, mellowed. Caffeine was another thing. Everything became expectant, taut. Waves of energy would travel from her mouth right to the delicate folds of skin at her center. She felt the heightened sense of prickly awareness. Every nerve, every surface suddenly there, present.

She stretched, the caffeine shooting out past her fingernails. Their eyes met a third time. Her stomach clutched. She smiled quickly and looked down.

She should go over there. Everyone she met through NYU was either too young or too gay. Maybe he spoke French? He looked like he could be Moroccan. Those rich black curls, the noir shadow. She thought of his lips forming French words and shivered. He wasn't a tourist—there was no camera or guidebook. A businessman? An architect? There was certainly power in those hands. A force. Or maybe that was the thing in the room between the two of them, vibrating over the empty chairs and tables and the perfect undisturbed place settings.

He was gesturing to Silvio. Whispers. Eyes flashed in her direction. Her stomach clutched again, this time harder. Was he asking something about her? Would Silvio be able to tell him anything? She strained to listen without looking as if she was. Before she could catch a phrase, a word, Silvio quickly left. She watched as the man stared off in the distance and absentmindedly traced the edges of the saucer, slowly, so slowly. She imagined her nipples under the pad of his finger. They hardened in response, and she covered herself. Silvio was again at her side. This time with a double espresso.

She glanced across the room at him. An offering or a dare? she wondered. She traced the top of the cup, mimicking his actions, savoring the pause, the effect it might have on him. She took a breath, raised her eyebrow, then the cup. "*Sahtein,*" she said, louder and bolder than before.

"*Aiesh.*"

Each sip was a rush of jittery urgency. She squirmed in her seat. Sound became amplified. Somewhere off in the kitchen silverware crashed and cooking oil exploded. She stole another fleeting look at him. He was tapping his foot in a rushed staccato rhythm. Tap-tap-tap-tap-tap-tap-tap. Each time she saw a flash of his exposed ankle. His skin. Skin that would lead to the ropey muscles of his calf, the delicate curve of the back of his knee, the warm trail of his inner thigh. A wave of sensation traveled down to her genitals.

"Silvio," she called over to him a little too loud, a little too shrill.

"Yes, miss. The check?"

"No, no. Not yet. A triple espresso. Two." There was a pause.

He came over to her, all kneading hands and furrowed brow. "No, no. You must not. You will be sick."

"Please. Two triples. One for me and one for the gentleman."

They held each other's gaze while the machine buzzed in the background. When the espressos arrived in large cups instead of the usual small ones, neither bothered with a toast. Their eyes never moving, never closing, they drank together in one continuous motion. She felt a burning, a sparkling. Angles jumped out at her. One move and she was going to leap up and project herself at him. Her heart pounded in her throat, behind her eyes. It was coming through the top of her head.

With great control, he slowly wiped the corners of his mouth, pushed back his chair, and rose up. He was tall, solid, taller than she had thought. Six feet three at least. She took in the gunmetal, pressed-linen pants. The faux cowboy buckle. The watch with the frayed red band, the silver emblem around his neck. His realness startled her. There was specificity. He existed.

He was walking toward her. There was a mole at the base of his chin, a vein that pulsed in his neck, a peek of chest hair—the green of a tattoo? A thin scar on his right wrist. She opened her mouth to speak. He brushed past her.

The hair on her arm stood up in his wake. She turned around in spite of herself. There he was, looking back again, fixing her with that hint of a smile. Was that an ever so slight movement of his head, motioning her back?

He slipped into the bathroom. The door closed behind him. She didn't hear the click of the lock.

She was standing before she knew she had done it. She should take her purse. Should she take her purse? People still did this. Would Sophie? Would she ever think to make the move from observer to participant? She took out her wallet. She put it back. She picked up her whole bag again. Was Silvio watching? Was his daughter? She smoothed back her hair. She walked tentatively to the door, stood there, shifted uncomfortably from one foot to another. He could be getting sick, for all she knew. He would come out and see her standing there, expecting—she would go to the ladies' room. She moved in that direction. Behind her she heard the click of the door opening. Before she could turn, a hand encircled her waist and pulled her inside, into the dark.

Thick mouths, warm, bitter lemon. Stubble. His hair rich, thick, wiry, on her cheek, her neck, her chest. She felt for the nape of his neck, searched for the elastic. The smooth of his skin. She had to feel it, all of it all at once. He unbuttoned her blouse, tore at her bra. His chest, the same bristly wiriness. She pressed herself flat against him. His hair tumbled around her, around her shoulders, down her cleavage. His hair, her hair. A smell of espresso and a deep male muskiness. She ran her hand down the front of his pants and felt him push toward her.

The clicking of belts unloosened. He backed her against what must have been the paper-towel dispenser. It hit her, hard and metal. A throbbing through her shoulder. But the pain felt good. Real.

He pulled off her skirt, pushed aside her panties, grasped a fistful of her pubic hair. That delightful pleasure of pain. Her hip hit the cold of the sink as he lifted her. It would leave a mark. Good, she thought.

She dug her nails into his shoulder blades. She wanted to bite his ear, pull his hair, steal a lock of it that she could take home with her.

He thrust into her suddenly with the whole of himself. She grabbed his shoulders, took him in deeper, their skin touching, mixing. She arched her neck. She heard the smash of something falling, crashing to the floor. She wanted to break everything, feel the shards, bleed, pull, tear. He felt so full. Intense. Rich. Bitter. Sweet. Smooth. Thick. Deep. Silky. "Ohhhhhh." The ripples began to take her. Wave after wave, the whole of him, her ass, his ass, his back, her nipples, her ribs, her collarbone.

Her hair had come loose. She was pinned to the wall by it, by his hand. He anchored himself against her, his hair falling lightly across her nipples, his breath in her right ear. He took the whole of it into his mouth, bit her hard. That exquisite pain. She cried out, heard his breathing change. Faster, harder, felt the muffled bursts of breath in her ear, the pull of her hair, her bare bottom smacking against the cold of the sink. She grabbed him deeper from inside herself, felt him pulse even harder.

There was a sudden knock on the door. They twisted quickly, careened off the sink, and landed with several thumps and thuds in a splayed heap on top of one another. "Hello! Hello! Are you all right in there?" A woman's voice—Silvio's daughter? She opened her mouth. "Someone's—" Fingers were softly on her lips stopping her. She breathed sharp pounding breaths. "Is someone in there? Hello?"

They waited interminably in the corner, hearts beating quickly together. Finally, he pulled her up. She reached for him just as she heard the quick zip of his pants. She crouched on the floor, tried to feel her way to her skirt. Where was it? She patted around hopelessly in the dark.

She reached for the light. He put his hand over hers, engulfing her as he had the cup. She listened to his breath. Felt his rapid heartbeat in her back. Took in the smell of sex. He burrowed his nose in her hair, found her neck with his lips. She wrapped her left arm silently behind him.

He slid by her and opened the door tentatively, just a crack. She could see the shadow of his sideburns, the thin glisten of sweat. He turned to her. "Lock it," he said.

He slipped out and was gone. She heard the click of the door closing. The retreating footsteps.

She waited, catching her breath.

He had said it with perfect clarity and understanding, without any trace of an accent: "Lock it." Not a phrase someone who didn't speak English would know. Her mind reeled. Knock-knock-knock. She crouched in the corner, waited like a naughty child.

Finally, she felt for the light and turned it on. She tried to make sense of her hair, her blouse with the missing button, the red from where he had held her at her collarbone. She shakily put on lipstick. Her eyes fell on the shards of the broken little vase under the table that was next to the toilet. She grabbed some paper towels, knelt on the floor, and picked up the pile. She went to transfer it to the sweet-looking floral wastebasket. At the last minute, she pushed it into the bottom of her purse.

When she came out, he was gone. His place was reset. The chair was flush with the table.

She sat back down, smoothed back her hair. She picked up Josie's paper. Her hands were shaking. What page had she been on, again? *The bride is an object of fear.* Right. She opened her pen. *Others consider her the goddess of lust or a symble for impulsive desire.* She circled the word. *Unique rules of physics and myth which describes the...* Physics? What was she talking about? It wasn't even a sentence. Her eyes slid down the page, barely taking in a word, an idea. They came to rest on a quote from Duchamp himself: "*The creative act is not performed by the artist alone; the spectator brings the work in contact with the external world by deciphering and interpreting its inner qualifications—*"

She was doodling. Red looping swirls lined the page of Josie's text. She crossed it out quickly, then put down her pen.

She should go do this at home. She could use the walk. Her mind and body still buzzed and zipped and soared with—what was it? Six cups of espresso? She should go to the gallery first in this state. She could probably walk there—all what was it, five miles? She would finish hanging the show in a mere half-hour.

"Check," she said, signaling to the busboy and silently thanking the powers that be that Silvio was nowhere to be seen. He was probably embarrassed or horrified for her. She thought of the broken vase in her purse. She would have to find a new place to grade papers first thing next week.

She stacked Josie's paper with the others, stood up, and began to put all of them in her bag when something caught her eye. She pulled Josie's paper loose again, folded it back to its cover. At the top of the page was a large, scrawled mark. The hurried hand of a man. "*A*," it said.

PEEPING TOM, DICK, AND HARRIET

Michelle Houston

"Explain to me again how this is supposed to be fun," I said as I surveyed the room, my hands on my hips. I tried not to show my dismay but knew I was failing. The room was painted battleship gray and reeked of disinfectant.

"Stacie, you're a closet exhibitionist. I thought it was time you come out and play for a bit. But in a safe way."

Great, another closet I needed to come out of. When I met Amy I was still a closet lesbian. It took less than three weeks for her to drag me out. I knew when I was beat down. She might be short and slender, but she was tenacious.

As she moved about the small room, placing candles on the floor and draping a furry blanket over the platform, which was the only form of furniture in the room, I began to get her idea. All around the room were windows—ten in all, with black slats covering them. Soon, a person would be behind each window. Customers who had paid would watch the slats go up and see into the room where we were standing. This was so they could watch us make love. There was no way for us to see into the rooms. Each window was a two-way mirror. They could see in, but we couldn't see out. It would give the illusion of privacy.

I had visited peeping booths before, but always from the other side.

"How long do we have?"

Amy lifted her wrist and glanced at her watch. "The owner said he would start letting people in at six o'clock. We have about five minutes."

Not a lot of time, but there wasn't a lot to do, either. While I had been lost in thought, she had worked to transform the room. It was still daunting and drab.

My libido wasn't registering that fact. As soon as it had clicked that people would be watching us, my panties had grown very, very wet.

"So what do I do?" I muttered.

Amy tossed a look over her shoulder, her long black hair falling down her back. I wanted nothing more than to wrap my hands in it and pull her head back, then lick and suck the slender column of her throat.

"Whatever comes naturally."

Looking down at my outfit, I knew Amy had chosen well. With a tight leather skirt, thigh-high boots, and a micro-mini lace tank top, all my assets were on display, including my belly-button ring and the dragon tattoo on my shoulder. My breasts strained against the lace top, making the outlines of my nipple rings stand out. It gave the impression that I was the butch in the relationship, even if I didn't really think of myself as such.

In contrast, Amy was dressed demurely in a simple corset top and long, flowing peasant skirt. The very one I love to hike up around her waist when I mount her with a strap-on from behind, while she leans over our balcony. Her corset was pale pink, contrasting perfectly with her deep-chocolate skin.

The lights flickered overhead, and I glanced at Amy in surprise.

"Showtime," she whispered and lay down on the black-and-white tiger-print throw she had used to cover the platform. She spread her legs and crooked her finger at me, inviting me closer as I heard the clapping of one set of slats go up.

Stepping forward, I moved into the V of her thighs and lowered myself tight against her. Her mouth covered mine, hungry. Her dainty hands grabbed my ass, pulling me tighter. Moaning softly, I cupped her breasts, pushing them over the top of her corset.

The clicking of another slat opening caused me to jerk, and Amy whispered, "Relax" into my mouth before sliding her hands under my skirt. Pulling it up, she worked her nimble fingers on the ties that held my panties up and soon had me naked from waist to mid-thigh, where my boots started.

I moved back so that she had room to pull off her skirt. Then she leaned back once more, spreading her legs wider. Her pussy was gorgeously bare and freshly shaved. I could see and smell her arousal. Bending over her, I licked along the bottom edge of her corset while she guided me to mount her mouth. Her tongue flicked along the seam of my pussy, and my focus blurred.

Across the room, another slat went up. I looked directly into the mirrored surface. I knew that in the tiny room someone was watching us, likely masturbating That's why we were on the stage. I imagined that I could almost see the outline of a hand fisted around a cock or a finger rubbing a clit. Would she have her legs thrown over the arms of her chair, her pussy spread wide?

The window next to it was revealed, and my mind started playing games. In that room was a couple, the woman seated on the man's lap, riding him while they watched us.

Beneath me, Amy was a tease, sucking at my clit, driving me wild, then blowing softly on my inner thighs. Unable to deny myself any longer, I leaned farther down and nipped softly at Amy's mound of Venus, slowly working my way down to her clit. I bit down, sending her arching against me, her slender body undulating on the print throw.

I could feel the telltale tremors moving through Amy's body. She was nearing orgasm, and if I didn't slow down the show would be over before it had begun. Moving back, I drew a gasp of surprised protest from her. I rolled off the makeshift bed and grabbed the bottom of the tank top and stripped it off. My miniskirt quickly followed, leaving me naked but for my black leather boots.

Reaching for her bag, I quickly found what I was looking for—my double-headed strap-on. Amy grinned and rolled over onto her hands and knees. She crawled to the other end of the platform. Turning around, she exposed her pussy to me and whoever was in the outer rooms.

Thrusting two fingers deep, she manipulated her pussy while I stepped into the harness and slid the fake cock into place. Stalking around the stage, I stroked my hand up and down the latex shaft, discreetly coating it with the KY I had squirted into my palm. Although I knew Amy's pussy was well lubricated—I could smell her heady scent in the tiny room—I wasn't planning on starting there.

Climbing on the platform, I moved to kneel behind her and grabbed a fistful of hair, jerking her head back roughly. Amy moaned as she arched against me, her breasts thrust out, rubbing along the edge of the corset. Alternately cupping them in her free hand, she pinched her nipples while I guided my cock to rest in the cleft of her ass.

"Yes," she gasped as I pressed harder against her, the tip of the cock working into her ass.

Applying pressure, I pushed forward, slowly pumping my hips until I was about halfway in. I could hear the squishing of her fingers as she thrust them harder into her pussy. Slats dropped down over windows only to quickly flip up again. That was a signal of applause—our audience approved.

Driving deeper, I had her squealing, her petite frame arching tight against me as she begged for more.

I wrapped an arm around her waist, joining her fingers with two of mine, thrusting them deep into her pussy as I seated my cock all the way in. Double mounted, she was in a state of high ecstasy, her body trembling and undulating in my arms, almost dislodging me.

Each jerk of her body sent the smaller cock, nestled within my own pussy, deeper and drove the tickler at its base across my clit. Spreading my legs wider, I pulled her back against me until she sat on my lap, her legs on either side of mine. My knees held her wide as I wiggled my hips, sending her into a small orgasm.

As she thrashed against me, gasping my name, I untied the laces on her corset and pulled it off, tossing it across the room.

Her hand left her pussy as I added another finger, then a fourth to quickly replace her own. She raised her soaked fingers to her mouth and sucked her juices from each digit slowly as I manipulated her pussy and clit, causing her to work her ass up and down on my cock.

I wanted to come, but at the same time I never wanted it to end. People were watching us get off and were getting off themselves. Already I could feel the urge to take it a step further, to fuck her in one of the clubs that catered to scenes. I could see her strapped to a Saint Andrew's cross, where I would first paddle her ass until she wouldn't be able to sit for a week without remembering it, then I would untie her and make her kneel and lick me off before I would let her come.

The imagery was intoxicating and brought a rush of excitement the likes of which I had never imagined. But she had. Somehow, Amy had known.

Pulling her back, I sank my teeth into her neck, biting the tendon that ran along the column of her throat, drawing a gasp from her. She jerked against my hand, her pussy juices coating it.

Around the room, the slats continued to fall and quickly rise, which increased our momentum. Pumping hard into her ass, I could feel her inner muscles clenching tight, holding my fake cock as she climaxed. Her body jerked and trembled. Her head whipped from side to side, her hair thrashing my face.

Although my nipples were tight with need and my pussy felt like it was about to explode, I still wasn't ready to come yet. I wasn't done with my show. As she sagged against me, her energy spent by the intensity of her orgasm, I pulled out of her and climbed off the platform.

After unbuckling the harness, I let it fall to the floor and moved to the first window. I stood facing it a few inches away, thrusting two fingers deep into my pussy. The tattoo on my mound rippled, making the fairy wings move as the flesh underneath jerked with the force of my movements.

Once I was sure my fingers were good and coated, I slipped them free. Rubbing them all over my breasts, I moved several steps to the side and repeated the process until I had given an up-close-and-personal show to each window.

Moving back to the center of the room, I stood there, legs wide, as I fingered myself. I almost lost my balance as a delicate hand slid up my thigh. I leaned over and gripped the platform with my other hand for balance, and I fucked my pussy until I felt my orgasm building, while Amy's hot tongue blazed trails of fire up my thighs, licking up my cream. Bending my knees, I added a third finger and pumped hard, until my orgasm crashed over me. I could feel my juices trickling down my inner thighs and Amy licking as fast as she could to catch every last drop. I continued to thrust my fingers into my gripping pussy until the last tremors ended and rational thought returned.

The lights flickered and all the slats dropped down.

I stepped into Amy's welcoming embrace, and together we climbed onto the platform. As we held each other, a voice came over the intercom asking if we were free for the same time the following Saturday. Seems our little show had drawn quite a few comments. Lifting my head, I looked down into my lover's warm, brown eyes.

"Thank you," I whispered.

Amy winked as I told the bodiless voice that we were definitely free for the next Saturday. Then I leaned down and pressed a soft kiss on Amy's lips.

UNDOING THE LACES

Andrea Dale

I hadn't really wanted to go camping. I never do. I'm less of a roughing-it type and more of a room-service type. But my husband and I do historic reenactment—dressing up in medieval clothes and hitting each other with sticks—so camping is a necessary evil.

By the end of this particular weekend, though, I had to rethink my position on the issue.

Because we haven't splurged on the big period pavilion, Greg and I are usually relegated to the "slums" on the outskirts of the encampment with the other modern tents. Which is fine. Our cabin tent is easy to put up and take down, which means we can throw our stuff inside, change into garb, and get down to having fun.

Plus, summer was lazing into autumn, and there wouldn't be many more perfect weekends with brilliant, clear, blue skies and mellow temperatures.

We'd joined the period dance revel on the second evening,

then done the rounds of the various campside parties. Thirsty from the whirling and spinning, I'd indulged in more homemade mead than I usually do. Which was why I was finding my way to the nearest Porta-Potty several hours after most everyone else had tamped down their fires and crawled into their sleeping bags. Oh, I could still hear some drumming and laughter in the distance, but those were the real die-hards.

I wasn't drunk, just pleasantly tipsy as I finished my business. My eyes had adjusted to the darkness, so I didn't bother to turn on my flashlight to go back to our tent. Of course, that meant I had to walk with more care so I wouldn't step on someone's armor that had been left out to air or trip over a tent rope.

Which may be why I noticed the light in our friends Kelly and Brad's tent, which was pitched next to ours.

I was pretty sure they'd just gotten back from their own evening of carousing. I opened my mouth to make some comment about their partying ways when I heard something.

Kelly's low, breathy moan.

The sound throbbed straight into my clit. My belly contracted. It was the most erotic thing I'd ever heard. (Porn was fine for porn's sake, but there's nothing sillier than all those fake moans and groans, especially when they happen while the actress's mouth is full of cock.)

This was real. An honest sound of blatant passion.

Holding my breath, I eased open the zipper to our tent, one tooth at a time, and crept inside, repeating the careful process to close the flap behind me. The nylon of the tent crackled as I slipped back into the double sleeping bag on the air mattress.

"Did you hear something?" Kelly asked, sounding vague and distracted.

"Nah. Everyone's asleep," Brad whispered back. "No, leave the light on."

"Won't somebody see?"

"They're all asleep," Brad repeated. "And I want to see you." His voice was rough with lust.

Although I'd never thought of myself as a voyeur, right now I wanted to see, too. On my knees, I peered out the half-moon window in the side of our tent, which we'd unzipped to let in the soft night air and the comforting scent of wood smoke. I could see easily through the screening.

With the light on in their tent, I couldn't so much see Brad and Kelly as I could their silhouettes. Again, somehow it was sexier than seeing their fully naked forms.

Her head was tilted back, and he was kissing her throat, his mouth moving languidly down the slender column to the curve of her breasts. From her shape, I could tell she was still wearing her corset. The outline of a crumpled heap in the corner must have been her dress, carelessly tossed aside when passion took over for common sense and care for the handmade garment.

My breasts felt heavy. I brushed my hand across them. My nipples were hard beneath my linen nightdress.

I eased down into the sleeping bag and reached inside. Greg was wearing just a pair of thin drawstring pants. I cupped my palm around his flaccid cock through the linen and, as quietly as I could, whispered for him to wake up.

I had no idea whether it was my hand or my voice that actually woke him. I didn't really care, as long as he could share this with me.

He started to speak, but I shushed him, barely breathing as I told him to sit up and look.

"Holy...Brad and Kelly?"

I nodded.

"We probably shouldn't watch," I whispered. "But...I want to..."

At first, Greg didn't say anything. Then, "Tell me why."

I squirmed inwardly; I wasn't always comfortable talking about how I felt in bed. But right now I was too horny to care.

"It's hot," I said honestly. "It's turning me on." To punctuate his words, I took his hand and showed him how my nipples were trying to poke holes through the weave of my nightdress.

I heard his sharp intake of breath. In the darkness, his eyes were like black pools of desire.

In the other tent, Kelly shifted position, kneeling facing away from Brad. Her head was bowed slightly, and I understood a moment later why when Brad lifted her thick hair and commenced nibbling at the back of her neck.

I heard long exhalation, her almost indistinct, "Mmm, yes."

My skin tingled in empathy. "Yes," I echoed.

Beside me, Greg slid his hand up my back to the nape of my neck. My hair was in a pair of braids, leaving the sensitive area exposed. I shivered as he trailed his fingers across my flesh. I would have loved to feel his mouth there, but I knew he wanted to watch, too.

That aroused me even more.

Now Brad began to unlace Kelly's corset. He didn't rush, pulling the long laces through the eyelets with excruciating slowness. As each inch of flesh was exposed, he bent and pressed his lips there, making a ritual out of the undressing.

Unbearably erotic.

As the corset fell free and the silk chemise beneath slid down, Kelly's breasts tumbled out, unrestrained. Kelly reached up, cupping her heavy mounds in her hands. She circled her nipples with her fingers, and I heard her whimper with pleasure.

"Do that," Greg said.

I stripped my now-confining nightdress over my head and

caressed my own breasts. Not as large as Kelly's but ample enough, and my nipples were delightfully sensitive.

Which Greg knew. "Pinch them," he said.

I couldn't see distinctly what Kelly was doing, but I could extrapolate. Hell, by this point, I didn't entirely care what exactly Kelly was doing. It was amazingly hot to watch, but I was desperate to feel, too.

My nipples sent electric signals to my clit, and as I played with myself, my hips pumped gently, moving to the primal rhythm of my fingers and my blood. Pleasure, a hint of pain, a throb of sensation.

Greg grazed his teeth across my bare shoulder, watching me, watching Kelly and Brad. My pussy felt swollen, slick.

Needy.

I abandoned my nipple and reached down, but Greg caught my wrist, guiding my hand to his crotch. He was rock hard, and he hissed between his teeth when I curled my fingers around him. I let go long enough to pull the drawstring bow free, then snaked my hand inside his pants to stroke him freely. Hot flesh, steely length. I couldn't remember the last time he'd been so hard. My thumb slipped through the bead of precome at his tip.

I brought my hand to my mouth to taste it, rubbing the sweetness against my lower lip.

For a moment it seemed as though the tables had turned, as if Kelly and Brad were somehow channeling us. Kelly turned, and I saw that I'd missed Brad stripping out of his pants—or maybe he hadn't been wearing them all along and only now he'd turned to full profile and I could see his cock jutting up.

Kelly turned, and bent to take the proud length of him in her mouth.

My hand went back to Greg, and he clenched his fist around mine. Too much sensation; he didn't want to come, not just yet.

Neither, it seemed, did Brad. He pulled Kelly up, caressing her shoulders, her breasts, sliding his hands down into the indistinct area between them. Kelly squealed under her breath. My pussy clenched, wanting that.

A fumble of movement in the other tent, but clear enough to us. Brad sat facing Kelly, and she straddled him, sinking down on him while he nuzzled her breasts. He leaned back on his hands, and she rocked back and forth on him. He had a great view.

So did we.

Greg shifted behind me. He was on his knees, and he drew me back toward his lap. I spread my legs, straddling him as well, only backward. Our knees would no doubt regret this in the morning, but right now, we didn't care.

All I cared about, certainly, was the feel of the length of Greg's cock sliding up inside of me. I bit my lip to keep myself from making too much noise. God, he felt so good inside me, filling me.

We couldn't really move much, not if we didn't want to be overheard. I suspected Kelly and Brad were so intent on their own rutting that they wouldn't have heard a phalanx of Roman guards rattle by, but I didn't want to take that chance, and neither did Greg.

Kelly's thrusts grew erratic. Greg, watching over my shoulder, reached around me to stroke his fingers against my clit.

Kelly had been whimpering, deep in her throat, as she obviously tried to keep quiet. Now the sound changed to a squeal. She clutched Brad's shoulders—I imagined her nails were digging into his back—as the sound rose in pitch.

The sights, the sounds, the feel of Greg's cock inside me and his fingers expertly teasing my clit—all sent me over the edge.

I stuffed my fist in my mouth to keep myself from screaming.

Distantly, I was aware of Brad hoarsely swearing and telling Kelly how much he loved her.

Greg jerked only once, twice. I clenched around him as he pulsed, my orgasm triggering his, Kelly's and Brad's orgasms triggering ours.

The next morning, as we were packing up our cars, I swear I saw Brad wink at Greg.

Yep, I might need to rethink my reluctance about camping.

CRUISING

Lee Cairney

When I'm getting ready to go out on the prowl I often get a feeling like the excitement of being sick—but without the nausea, like my stomach lining is trying to peel away. It feels good in the same way that inhaling sherbet up your nose feels good, and believe me, I do mean good. I pull on my heavy, steel-capped biker boots, tucking them under my leather trousers, and sling my battered, black leather jacket over my white vest. One large silver spike rivets my ear. My hair is dark and cropped short, snug against my head. I was once told that I had eyes like flakes from an iceberg—whatever that means. I'm wearing bondage cuffs, tight confections of soft, supple leather and stainless steel, around both wrists for the constriction and sheer pleasure of it. I know I'm looking good.

I bang the door behind me and stroll down the hill from my apartment. I live in an ancient cathedral city where small, beautiful medieval churches cluster and old flint-faced walls run into each other. Beautiful, but it's difficult to find the sex I need in this small, provincial place. I walk to the riverside, leaving little trails of icy breath in the dark air behind me. Dirty water slaps against the moorings and a line of grubby, white cruising boats. I slouch my shoulders forward just a tiny bit and check that my jacket covers my small tits. It does. I step across the toll bridge and into the wooded park that marks the beginning of the local cruising area for gay men. I've become used to getting my kicks vicariously. I enjoy the ambiance. Strange men stalk between the trees, crunching leaves underfoot. Some of them walk dogs and feign nonchalance. I've even seen a few round here in business suits—no doubt, their wives are left waiting at home as they sully loafers in the mud and snag holes in pinstripe, rubbing against the rough bark of a tree as they're taken brutally and swiftly by a faceless man they met twenty seconds before.

A whole new language of looks and come-ons develops. Rejection is as subtle as the tilt of a head. Tonight, the air is spiced with the smoky tang of autumn and a sharp, slowly trickling sense of muted danger. Dark parkland, bushes, and trees lie ahead of me. Often, I catch men fucking and stand and watch them—on their hands and knees, being shunted hard from behind, or half hidden by a bush as a thickening cock rams into their warm mouths, or even sitting on one of the forgotten park benches stroking each other's dicks.

Walking soundlessly, I reach the center of the park, continually checking the shadows and the real obstacles that appear in my path. My clit is tingling. It aches from the recent sight of a youngish-looking man being fucked in the arse by a heavy, blond man in biker's leathers, whilst twisting his head around at the same time to service the throbbing, red-tipped erection of another, kneeling man. I had to force myself to steal quietly away before they shot down his throat and arse, worried I'd forget myself and betray my presence by some involuntary noise of lust and envy mixed together. Now, just ahead of me I see the outline of a tall, slim shape leaning against a tree. I prepare myself to walk casually past, but my heart is bumping in my chest cavity. For the first time tonight, I feel like I'm on display. The man is dressed in dark clothes—jeans and a jacket, perhaps—and is leaning with one foot up against the tree. Something dangles from his right hand—oh, it's a dog leash. I relax slightly. I'm close enough to see that his hair is cut even shorter than mine. I look around but can't see the dog.

"Hey," the figure murmurs softly, and I follow the sound without any real thought. I'm standing opposite now, face to face. For all my five feet seven, I feel short. A pleasurable sensation freezes my brain as the dog owner reaches forward with leather-gloved hands and manipulates me so I'm facing the tree. I'm pushed so hard against it that I can feel the patterns of the bark pressing into my cunt. Hypnotized, I stay pressed against the thick trunk while the leash is used to fasten my hands together around the other side, securing me tightly to the tree.

"Cuffs—convenient," a concentrating voice mutters from the other side of the tree. The burning, stretching sensation in my arms as the final knot is tied restores some of my sense to me.

"What are you doing?" A pathetic and useless question. The dog owner suddenly slams against me from behind, shoving me hard and nearly winding me.

"You should be quiet. I'm going to expose you...play with you...do what I like with you. If you want to be freed at the end, don't make it necessary for me to use a gag or blindfold."

I stop squirming and trying to turn my head to see over my shoulder. That and my heavy breathing are taken for assent. All I can think is how I can now feel breasts against my back, and something harder, lower. The voice, although gruff, isn't quite low enough to be a man's, I realize. I can't believe it.

A cold, gloved hand reaches round and flips open the buttons of my trousers. Then my trousers are dragged down round my ankles. My assailant—whom I now know to be a woman—hoists my vest and jacket into a bundle around my shoulder blades. The chill air is like a slap to my whole body. My skin creeps up into gooseflesh. I'm naked, exposed, tied to a tree. I wonder how many people can see the luminous white of my flesh in the darkness, watching me just as I watched them. Leathermen, big daddies, bikers, circling around me with their cocks out, stroking them to hardness.

I can feel the zip of her jeans and the hard metal of her belt buckle pressing into my bare arse and burning with the cold. Her hands reach round and grab the erect tips of my nipples as my legs are kicked apart—as wide as the trousers shackling my ankles will allow. She just spreads me wide and helps herself. My nipples are being plucked and pinched and teased into aching points of chafed skin. Then the pressure against my arse recedes, and all my thoughts are concentrated in my nipples being worked so hard and grazed against the rough skin of the tree.

My cunt is dripping wet as I feel the cold tip of something long and very thick pressing tantalizingly against it. I try to open my legs wider but fail, and I let out a visceral grunt of frustration. The freezing silicone head is rubbed up and down across the opening to my cunt, nudging up to my erect clit and slowly back down again to rest against the tight pucker of my arsehole.

"Maybe I should take you right here," she says, "like the little gay boy that you are, cruising around in the woods, looking for sex. Well, you've found it."

The head of her dick pushes against my clenched arsehole.

"No," I hear myself saying, "I've never been taken there." Can't she read the signs? I'm a top. I do not take it up the arse.

"Forbidding me, are you?" she croons. "We'll see."

Before I can reply she slams the thick dick she's packing into my cunt. Opening and stretching me, she gives my tight hole no time to adjust to the length and thickness. My cunt aches as she rams against the top of my cervix with her blunt, thick head, pulling nearly all the way out of me before thrusting back deep inside me. All I can feel is her in my cunt and her leather and metal bruising my buttocks. Anger at my enforced and unusual passivity and the sheer force of her cruel and energetic pounding begin to warm me.

I'm spread-eagled, wrapped around a tree, and helpless. The muscles in my arms and stomach are being pulled to unbearable tautness as she works on me. I simply have to stand, spread and open, and let her impale my cunt repeatedly. I feel like I'm actually going to split down the middle but, despite myself, I can't help trying to push against her insistent, plunging dick.

"Oh, do you want some more?" She grabs me by the half-inch of hair on my head. "I'll give you what you want."

Her dick slicked wet from my cunt, she pulls it back and then pushes it into my virgin arse. It hurts like hell, more than sherbet up your nose. This is definitely a boundary. I feel like I'm going to dissolve, that I can't possibly bear her plunging in and out with long, hard strokes, or that I'll explode. But my sphincter tightens around every move she makes.

"That's right. Milk my good, big dick."

I'm just about to start screaming when her hand works its way round and insinuates itself against my clit. The cool leather strokes against my hard clit as she fills my arse again and again. I can't hold back, and with my arse and clit being worked hard and my cunt empty and swollen to the night air I come so hard that all I can see is the rushing of red blood tissue before my eyes. It feels like she's come inside me, violating me further, flooding my walls, but I know this can't be true as it's only her silicone dick that is now being edged slowly out of me.

I sag against the tree as she plays the point of a knife up and down, up and down over my exposed flesh, before placing the handle in my hand. With difficulty I saw through the binding holding my wrists. Freed, I turn quickly round, rearranging my clothes. There is nothing but shadows and trees and bushes, a severed piece of leather, and the rushing of the cold night air.

ROOF FLASHING

Debra Hyde

Sure of his footing, Brady Williams pulled his knit hat as far down over his ears as possible, thankful that the wind had finally abated. Had it continued its rage of the previous hours, standing on the roof would have been impossible. Had it continued, Brady would not only find more damage but maybe frostbite as well. A plummeting temperature was aggravating enough, but wind chill was more than he had bargained for. And there was little enough on-the-job bargaining: When the hotel management said jump, you leaped. This time, leaping meant climbing atop the roof.

He had quickly spotted several areas void of singles on the north side of the roof, appreciative that the exposed underlying roofing felt, like black holes against the brilliance of heaven, stood out so well against the light-colored shingles. Here, he only had to document where damage had occurred, estimate the number of singles he'd need for repairs, and give the felt a quick check for tears and missing chunks. Fortunately, it had held up well. None of it flapped torn or loose.

The rest of his job, however, would not be so easy. Checking every area of flashing never was. It required stooping to inspect every spot of aluminum that shielded the base of every mortared chimney, every vent pipe, each valley that creviced where the various wings of the building met, and every drip edge and gutter. Whether step or continuous, every piece of roof flashing needed its look-see.

Brady steeled himself to his undertaking, determined to get the job done quickly but thoroughly. He ignored the grackles that clung to the branches of the tree just below him, cackling and flitting about as they feasted on the dried red berries that hung there. He ignored the comings and goings of hotel guests who slammed trunks and car doors and shouted after children wild with energy from too long a car ride. He tried to ignore the rumble of the highway, but the sounds of semis sputtering slower against the accelerating roar of fast-and-furious cars were too captivating to disregard. That's where he wanted to be—roaring along the lanes, outmaneuvering traffic—not here on a roof, braced against the cold.

I'm getting too old for this, he thought.

His gaze wandered with his thoughts—it always did, he knew—when motion caught his eye. It came from the neighboring hotel. The competition, his bosses called it. But when a woman moved before the window of her room, a thrill shot through him and opportunity seized him.

She was naked, gloriously naked. Slightly plump in her hips and stomach with breasts that sagged in seasoned wisdom, she moved, comfortable with her body. She had an obvious confidence, one that proclaimed it didn't matter how your body aged; if you liked sex, you put that body to good and pleasurable use.

Her poise made Brady's cock twitch, but when she reached

elsewhere and brought a dark clump of an item into view, his cock sprang to life, throbbing with awareness. His face burned with the blush of surreptitious discovery, but whatever his embarrassment, he could not look away. He *would* not look away.

Because when the woman stepped into the leather harness and cinched it around her waist, its intent clearly and visibly protruding, she held his deepest fantasy between her legs.

His was a long-held fantasy, discovered in younger days in much the same stealthy way as he watched the woman now. They had hung out "down the meadows" in those days, he and his friends. They had conducted their social life from the banks of the river, drinking beer, smoking pot, sometimes tossing a Frisbee across a sod field or casting a fishing line into the river, but mostly avoiding having to go home each night to their boring bedrooms, intrusive parents, and limited means until long after dark.

The lucky ones among them brought their girlfriends with them, and the luckiest among them had been Ray. Discharged from the military and slightly older than Brady and his buds, Ray came home with enough money in his pocket to buy a van and get a girlfriend. Both were beauties: the van for its airbrushed art, the girlfriend for her sweeping long hair, high cheekbones, and visible cleavage. Out of Ray's earshot, they had lusted after both with equal vim, but in his presence, they acted as mature and self-possessed as possible. Where they made asses of themselves in their own dismal company, they strove to be anything but in the presence of Ray and his stunning and vivacious girlfriend.

Brady watched the woman slather on lubrication and wondered if Ray's girl had used lube as well. He remembered that night, the night they had completely disregarded "if this van's a-rocking" protocol and tried to surprise Ray. They had spied

Ray's van north of their usual meeting place and, too stoned for their own good, their usual composure the victim of good weed, they had crept up on the van.

They had only wanted a glimpse of tit, Brady remembered, a hint of nipple. They had watched to glimpse the thrust of bodies in a heated fuck. They just wanted to see it, surprise Ray, and have a good laugh.

They should have stopped when they heard the cries. The noise had been too guttural, too animalistic, unfamiliar, and alien. It wasn't the passion of a woman taking it. But what had they known then?

Brady watched the woman approach her lover. He could only see the man's ankles, legs resting on a chair's seat, obviously kneeling there in presentation. His cock throbbed at the sight, prompting Brady to move along the roof until his angle revealed more of the man in waiting.

At best, he could only see the man's lower torso. With a bit of hang in the belly, the man was, like his partner, older, and Brady thought he glimpsed rope around the man's ankles. Damn but bondage made his cock ache.

The woman stepped up to the man, stood between his legs, and aimed. She pressed into him, parting him. The man flinched at first touch, then tilted his ass toward her.

He wants it, Brady thought. *He wants her cock. He wants her to shove it in and drive it home.*

He wondered if Ray had wanted it the same way, that night so long ago. He would never know, because Ray and his girlfriend had already been going at it. Oh, they saw tit and they saw fucking, but not the way they had expected it. Back then, Brady hadn't even conceived such a thing was possible. He knew better now.

She slid her cock into the man slowly, watching it disappear into his ass. Brady was surprised to see the man take it readily, his ass appearing to suck the cock into itself, and envied his apparent skill and expertise. He watched the cock reappear and then move in a cadence he was all too familiar with: Fucking. Fucking he knew and knew well, but he had never been as fortunate as Ray had in years past. He had never known the feel of a woman's cock up his ass; he had only longed for it ever since that night.

The woman smiled as she did her lover—an expression that sent a shiver through Brady—and when she laughed, his cock lurched so hard, it hurt.

"Bette," he called her. "Bette." He didn't know why he named her that, but he had to call her something. He had to name this miracle of a woman.

Bette pummeled her lover hard, ramming him like a porn star on a sport-fucking rampage. Her lover's ass trembled and pitched, every twitch and lurch reflecting just how intense this reaming was. Brady thought of all the porn he'd sought out in the years since the irate and embarrassed Ray had disappeared forever from his company. He had scoured every adult bookstore for anything that featured a woman who harnessed a cock. Most often, the fictional creature made men suck it, and she'd slap a face with it while uttering the most belittling curses imaginable. Once in a great while, he'd hit pay dirt, and she'd shove it up her male victim's ass.

Brady gripped himself, cupping his clothed erection in his gloved hand, thinking of one such domina, a vision that was nothing more than some artist's line art, as he watched Bette buck atop her lover. Brady thought of a JPEG, the first one he'd ever seen of a girl fucking a guy—two skinny, twentysomething youths, he with a long dick dangling, she with a harness and a hard-on; he on all fours in ass-presenting supplication, she on her knees, giving it to him. Brady still had that JPEG.

Bette pulled out of her lover and started to unbuckle.

No, Brady thought. *Not yet! It's too soon!*

She tossed aside the harness and freed her lover from the chair.

It's over. Damn, it's over.

Morose, bereft, Brady expected to move on—until he saw Bette take her lover to the bed and lay him down, on his side. She donned a glove (latex, Brady assumed) and squeezed lube onto her sheathed hand. She sat along side her lover, behind him.

And her hand disappeared.

She leaned toward her lover and spoke to him. Brady watched the man reach for his dick and did the same, but atop his pants. His fingers danced in small taps, a sorry variation upon a grand theme, but it was all he had there on the roof. He'd seen a voyeur masturbate this way in an S-M club once, and although gloves and heavy workpants prevented him from really feeling his effort, he'd take whatever stimulation he could get.

Bette, he knew, was working her lover's prostate. Bliss spread across the man's face in angelic, beatific expression. He looked like a saint whose torture had brought him into the pure light of heaven, there to wait suspended between earthly sensation and heavenly transcendence. But Brady knew this was hardly the thing of saints. He knew that this bliss was a thing most carnal. It was fingers intruding, pressing, and rubbing, a hand stroking hard flesh, a body rising in an all-too-human rapture.

Swiftly the man reached his climax. He pulled his ball sac taut, pinching it hard between his fingers. His strokes grew fast and furious, and the head of his cock had disappeared into the palm of his vast hand. Seeing her lover reach this state, Bette began to chant to him, and when Brady discerned her words, his own arousal leaped to such a height that he threw aside his gloves and opened himself to the elements.

Come for me. Come for me. Come, come. Come now.

Brady imagined how Bette sounded, voicing the words he had longed to hear all his life. Bette's lover was in the throes of it now, his face screwed tight, his body stiff, fluid spurting from a hand that pulled and milked, shuddering hard at the height of release, then quivering as his orgasm dribbled away.

Brady watched all this furtively, his freezing hand pumping. But when Bette leaned forward, kissed her lover's cheek, and murmured to him, Brady closed his eyes and spilled into his own ecstasy. He stiffened and let his peak rip through him. Spewing seed, he repeated Bette's command.

"Come for me. Come for me. Come for me. Come. Come... Come..."

The words rode tandem to his orgasm, strong in the initial rakes of spasm, fading as tension and relief melted from his body. It was an intense and satisfying orgasm, and when Brady opened his eyes, he saw Bette's glove tossed aside, her lover suckling her breast and his hand plowing between her legs.

He left them then, pushing his weary dick back in his pants, retrieving his gloves, and shoving his freezing, sticky-with-jism hands into them. He wished Bette well, still envied her lover, and thought of the shift's end when he'd return home and revisit what he had seen today. He'd recall Bette's every move, her lover's every reaction, whether pleasured or tense, and he'd do so with a favorite toy up his ass, its vibrations shooting against his prostate as he stroked himself.

Yes, he'd remember Bette, remember the fucking and the massage and the stroking. He'd remember her words, her commands, all the while praying for the day he'd meet his own Bette. He'd long for the day she'd appear, packing a strap-on, gloved, and ready. He'd ache for the feel of her tool penetrating and pumping. He'd beg her to ream him, rape him, ruin him.

Coming in his solitude, he'd cry out for her, his voice raised on high in a hope so strong that it would fly to the heavens where, perhaps, it might be heard. Where, perhaps, it might be answered. To which Brady mouthed a quiet amen, climbed down from the roof, and went his wishful way.

WATCHING

Dante Davidson

Zach is a bartender at a restaurant that's so hip it doesn't even have a name. There's only an address on the outer concrete wall. In order to get a job at 68 Paradise Street, you have to be outrageously good-looking. Zach fits the description. He's half German, half Native American, and he has deep green eyes and straight black hair that hangs past his shoulder blades. When he's clean, he's like a living dream, so spectacular you're not sure you're actually looking at a real person and not an airbrushed fantasy.

When he's dirty, he's mine.

I'm a representative for one of the bigger vineyards in Sonoma. We make very good wine, which means that I don't have a difficult job at all. I bring my samples to the best restaurants and pour out tastes for the owners. They always order. My life is sweet.

Sometimes, owners ask the opinion of their favorite employees when they choose wine. If Zach worked for you, you'd definitely ask his opinion. On wine. On food. On the way your hair smells. On the muscles that ripple across your stomach. On the position of your cock when it's hard. You'd get his opinion whenever you could. He's that kind of a guy. He makes you want to get close to him and hear him talk.

I met him on an afternoon at 68 Paradise when his young and rather pudgy boss asked if Zach would join us in a booth to taste my latest samples. Zach sat across from me. His green eyes watched me. His full lips mesmerized me. His handsome face made it difficult for me to remember my name or the name of my wine or the reason I was sitting there, or where I had to go later in the evening.

Luckily, my job comes naturally for me. I served the samples, sold my wares, and gave Zach my card. He surprised me by using it the same day, paging me, sending a shiver of anticipation through me that I hadn't felt in years.

It's not that I'm ugly or unused to the attention of attractive men. It's that I've never seen someone like Zach before. I'm fine looking, myself. Tall, in shape, with dark hair that's graying at the temples. I dress in expensive suits when I'm selling, and in faded jeans and crisp white T-shirts when I'm selling something else.

I have no problem getting laid.

But I wanted this one. I wanted him, not for a one-night stand but as a permanent fixture in my bedroom, over my kitchen table, on my balcony. And he called. He said he was intrigued. He apologized for staring at me in the restaurant, but said that I'd somehow managed to give him a raging hard-on while I spoke and he needed to see me.

This gave me the upper hand, somehow, and it allowed me to slow my beating heart and be the kind of man Zach requires. A tough man. A strict man. A strong man. A dom man.

He came over after his shift, at almost three in the morning. I was ready, not in the least bit tired, and I saw then what I know now. Zach is gorgeous when clean; after working for eight hours at the furious pace of a bar like 68 Paradise, he is...he is... No words describe it except "changed." His skin is warmer and it has the scent of manly sweat on it. His muscles are alive beneath the golden canvas of his body. His eyes are darker green than in the light of day. He changes the way a vampire changes. Daylight holds him in its spell. At night, he comes alive.

"Could I shower?" he asked. "I came right over from work."

"No," I said, shaking my head to punctuate my statement. "No. I like you like this. You're mine like this. I want you just to strip and stand there."

My apartment is done entirely in white. There is a white rug, white walls, white sofa. I don't like the fussiness of color. I like things stark. When Zach stripped and stood still in the center of my living room, it was as if he were a piece of art on display in a museum. I couldn't contain myself. I walked around him, observing him, not touching him yet but memorizing all parts of his body.

His cock was of mammoth proportions, beautifully crafted, hard as a piece of steel forced out and away from his body. He closed his eyes while I stared, but I told him to open them. He seemed at ease in his nakedness but confused by the way I was circling.

I said, "I've waited a long time for you. I want to learn how you look and work. I want to see you make yourself come so I can understand the changes in your face. I will educate myself on what you like and don't like. I will never forget what you need."

He didn't move.

I said, "You felt it at the bar and you know what I'm talking about. You and I are right for each other and I will control you and take you where you need to go. But as with any new purchase, the owner needs to read the manual. I want to know what you like and what it takes to make you come. You show me this one time, and I will never require a second lesson."

"You want me to jerk off?"

"Use your hand," I told him. "Use it the way you do when you're alone at home and it's been a long night and you need some release. Do it the way you've done since you were a teenager." I was talking through nearly gritted teeth; I don't know why. The sound of my voice was unrecognizable to me, almost monotone, but I didn't care.

I wanted to watch.

I needed to see.

He slowly wrapped the fingers of his right hand around his throbbing cock. I took my breath in and held it while he began to stroke himself. I've never seen anything quite as beautiful as the spectacle of him standing naked and pleasing me with his own personal pleasure. Each stroke was a chord inside my head, a cymbal, an electric jolt.

He grew more comfortable with me as his audience, and he closed his eyes and tightened his thigh muscles. I would have demanded he open his eyes at any other time, but if this was the way he did it at home, solo, then I wouldn't fight him on it.

His strokes grew faster and rougher, and I felt myself breathing hard and fast as if to match that speed. His hand became almost a blur, and the edge of his palm made a smacking sound against his skin each time he connected. It was something from an X-rated movie, something from my fantasy repertoire, something from a place older than time.

He sucked in his breath between his teeth right before he erupted. His head went back, and I wanted to go to him and hold him, but I was frozen where I stood, watching the come spurt from his cock, watching his hand slow, slow, stop.

I came forward, bent on my knees to taste the silvery liquid of sex. He looked down at me, dark green eyes aware again, losing their afterglow quickly.

And I watched.

NOT A VOYEUR

Alison Tyler

I'm not a voyeur," I told my boyfriend Courtney.

"I never said you were," Courtney murmured from behind the sports section of the newspaper. This was his favorite place to spend every Saturday morning.

"Really," I insisted. "I'm not."

"Why do you keep saying that, Lora?" he asked, sounding part bemused, part annoyed.

"Because of them," I told him, my voice low.

"Them, *who?*"

"Those people out there. *Fucking.*"

Courtney set down his paper. He looked at me with his great green eyes as I pointed out the window, at the apartment across the street, and at the people in the apartment who were screwing each other silly. Without a word, Courtney stood and came to my side, so that we were both pressed against our own window, looking out.

I heard him suck in his breath as he took in the vision.

The girl was tall with blond curls that fell past her shoulders and a tight, athletic physique. She looked like someone who never missed a workout. The man was well built, with thick red hair cut short and several vibrant tattoos decorating his muscular arms. He had the girl in a tight embrace, and he was lifting her up and sliding her down on his cock, over and over and *over*.

"Oh, man," Courtney murmured, gripping tightly onto my hand. "Just look at that."

I felt myself getting wetter as I watched. Apparently, the vision was having a similar effect on Courtney. Not that he was getting wetter, of course, but that he was getting hard. He took my hand and placed it over the bulge in his drawstring pajamas, and I sighed when I felt the hidden treasure there that awaited me. Well, not quite so hidden. He'd completely tented the thin plaid fabric.

"How long have they been doing that?"

"I don't know," I told him. "I wasn't watching. I'm not a voyeur, you know." I managed to sound just the slightest bit indignant.

"That's right," he agreed, nodding. "Neither am I."

"I just happened to look out the window. And there they were."

"Sure," Courtney said, understanding. "Could happen to anyone."

We stood in awed silence for several seconds until the man slid the girl off his cock and flipped her around. She was facing us now, and we both ducked instinctively.

"Do you think they can see us?" Courtney asked softly, as if the couple could not only watch our every move but hear our every whisper. He was on the left of the window now, and I was on the right.

"I guess so," I told him. "I mean, if we can see them, right?"

Cautiously, I peered back out the window. The girl was facing us, but she had her eyes closed, and the man was staring down at her. They didn't seem aware in the slightest that they were basically fucking in public. I wondered if they had forgotten to lower the blinds, or if they'd left them up intentionally, hoping someone might peek in.

"But they're not looking at us," I continued, moving back into place so I could watch. Courtney joined me immediately.

"No," he said, "they're definitely not."

"They're too busy," I continued.

"Yeah," Courtney nodded. "Busy."

The lovers were completely consumed by their actions. And who wouldn't be in their place? The fucking was so intense I could practically feel it. No, that wasn't right. What I was feeling was Courtney, who had moved behind me and wrapped me up in his strong arms, holding me tight so that his cock pressed against my ass. I sighed again and arched my back to let Courtney know what I wanted.

Even through his pajama bottoms and the flirty little pair of pink-polka-dot knickers I had on, I could feel that he was all the way erect. I wasn't surprised in the slightest when Courtney slipped one hand under my lace-trimmed panties to see if I was wet.

He came away with his fingers made slick by my juices. I could hear him licking his fingertips clean, and I shuddered, still staring at the couple, but only half seeing them. I was torn. I wanted to turn my head and watch Courtney taste my own sweet juices, but I didn't want to miss a frame of the action across the street.

Courtney brought his hand back to my pussy once more, this time overlapping two fingers and sliding them inside me. I groaned at the feeling of being worked by his hand, but while I normally would have shut my eyes to concentrate, now I forced myself to watch the couple across the way. Truly, I was having a difficult time figuring out who to pay attention to—the pretty couple or my handsome husband.

But why choose?

I could revel in the way Courtney touched me, and I could keep on staring out the window. Staring hard, because now the man was spanking the woman in time to his thrusts. Her mouth opened, and I could just guess that she was crying out, punctuating each smack with a deep groan. I thought her voice would be sexy and husky. Not a high-pitched squeal but a low, excited moan. Yet their window was closed, like ours, so I couldn't hear anything. I could only imagine the sounds.

"God, they're sexy," I said before I could stop myself. "Not that I'm *into* voyeurism or anything."

"Yeah," Courtney agreed, and then quickly added, "You know, I'm not a voyeur, either."

"Oh, I know that," I told him, feeling him step away from me. I turned my head, confused, and then realized he was simply taking off his pants.

"I've never even thought of watching people before," he said, moving on to his bright-red T-shirt.

"Of course not," I nodded, pulling my panties down my legs and stepping out of them, then slipping off my semi-sheer tank top. Totally naked, I took up my position in front of the window once more, knowing that Courtney was going to want to be behind. In this position, we could both stare at the neighbors and Courtney had easy access to me.

It's funny that we didn't even think of heading to the bedroom. There wasn't a question between us about where we were going to fuck or even if we *were* going to fuck. Courtney, who is always such a gentleman in bed, didn't even bother to ask if I was ready. He'd already felt for himself. He simply gripped onto my hips and slid forward, so that I could feel his cock drive all the way into me. He started off strong from the start, rocking me to the perfect rhythm, his hands on my hips moving me just the way he wanted.

Was it my imagination, or was he fucking me to the same beat as the couple across the way?

I sighed as I felt him slip one hand under my body to strum my clit. He always knows how to touch me so that the pleasure begins to spread throughout my whole body. But this time every sensation felt extra-intense. His cock was so hard. My pussy was so wet.

In fact, I was wetter than I'd been in a long time.

We've always enjoyed a good sex life. It was only in the past few weeks that work pressures had gotten to us. Why had we let our careers intrude? I had no idea. And I couldn't think of that right now, because something far more intrusive was on my mind. Courtney's intrusive cock, to be precise.

"Do you think they know we're watching, Lora?" he murmured, hot breath on my ear.

"I don't know. But I don't think they care. Or they'd have lowered the blinds."

"Some people forget how close they are to their neighbors," he reminded me. "They feel safe so high in the air. They forget other people might be watching."

"But not *us*," I reminded him. "Because we're not voyeurs."

"No," he agreed. "Definitely not us."

"We're just curious," I said, my breathing growing faster now.

"Curious," he repeated, as if that was the perfect word to describe what we were.

We were *so* curious, in fact, that we couldn't look away. We were hypnotized by the way the people across the street were making love. Mesmerized, until the pleasure began to build even stronger inside of me. Stronger with each thrust.

God, I love the way my man fucks me. His cock reaches all those most wonderful places inside. And when he grips into my hips, as he was doing now, I can hardly think at all. The spirals of arousal take over, and all I want to do is close my eyes, reaching that swoonlike state of total ecstasy.

But I didn't want to close my eyes today.

I wanted to watch that nubile blonde across the way. I wanted to see her play acrobatics with her red-haired boyfriend. Or husband. Or the stranger she'd met the night before.

Who was he? Who knew? And, really, who cared?

Courtney cared. "Do you think they're married?" he asked.

"I don't know." I was panting now, finding it not only difficult to think but difficult to breathe. I couldn't remember the last time I'd been this excited. Couldn't remember the last time we had fucked this intensely. Had we ever screwed in the kitchen before? No. Had we ever been in a window? Of course not.

"Maybe she met him online," Courtney said, spinning out a story. "Maybe they met for a drink last night at the bar on the corner, and then decided to live out their fantasy."

"What fantasy?"

"Fucking in public."

"They're not really in public."

"You're right," he said. "But they're close. Anyone in our building could be watching them."

"And anyone in *their* building could be watching *us*," I reminded him, and suddenly the fucking got harder. Suddenly, Courtney was moving me as fast as the man across the way was moving his partner. Suddenly, the intensity had ratcheted up another notch. I could tell from the way Courtney groaned that he liked the idea of people watching.

Who knew?

He'd never said anything about sex in public before. The most we'd ever done was hold hands, or kiss occasionally, pressed up against our favorite bar after closing time. But we'd never groped.

Never fondled.

Never fucked.

Yet now the thought of someone watching us pushed Courtney over the top, and he came calling out my name, slamming so hard into me. "Oh, God, Lora. Oh, my fucking God."

I pressed back on his cock, impaling myself on him, and as I shuddered and climaxed I realized that I liked the thought, too.

"I'm not an exhibitionist," I said softly as Courtney wrapped me up once more in his arms.

"Of course you're not," Courtney sighed. "Me, neither."

LIKE THIS

Rachel Kramer Bussel

When I first hear Tim's request, I'm not sure I can do it. It's one thing to spread my legs in the name of sex, to let him inside me, to show off my pussy to him as he's about to devour it, both of us so far gone we've practically melted into each other already. At those times, I know what I'm getting into, know we're about to join forces, merge our hot, needy bodies—pink, wet, warm flesh against pink, wet, warm flesh—sinuous and connected. I'll bend over any way he asks if he's going to touch me with those magic hands, that hot tongue, that powerful cock that he commands so well. That's easy for me because we're both moving, acting, doing. It's a ritualized mating dance, an erotic call-and-response, my signal followed immediately by his pounce.

I know exactly how powerful my pussy is to him, and how hungry he is for it, and I will gladly open wide to offer myself as his own private, sexual all-you-can-eat buffet. But even though we've been together since college, which I'm sad to admit is over a decade, showing him what I do on my own is different. That's my time, my space, my moment to go places I can only get to with the hum of my vibrator and my mind spinning to outer space. I've always needed personal privacy, both for solo sex and my sanity, pockets of time that are meant for me and me alone. I've never thought about how I look when I contort myself into all kinds of positions that make yoga look like skipping, spread my body in ways I'd have thought impossible until fueled by the rush of arousal.

With him, I have a little routine, though I'd never really thought of it that way before. He sits before me, and I spread my legs wide in the air, try to gracefully arch my strong thighs as my wetness glistens. I look up at him and often feel the creep of a blush tickle my cheeks. Sometimes I hold onto my ankles or, if I'm particularly limber, my heels, parting my legs as I think about his dick plunging inside. I smile at that special blend of lust and embarrassment as the scent of my arousal wafts its way upward to my nose. He waits patiently, even though I can see his hard cock, ready and raring to go. I run a finger up my slit, and feeling the wet, soft flesh there, truly feeling it deep inside, sometimes startles me. Tears start to form in my eyes as I do it again, and again, with one light, increasingly shaky finger until I gently part my lips, my thumbs doing the same for the hood. His eyes dart from my center to my soul, from my open lips to my open lips, taking me all in before he overtakes my body with his. I want to bare everything for him because I know he's about to enter me, to give me the one thing I can't give myself. I can get over my shyness because I can see, in an instant, how hard I've made him, and I know it's only a matter of time before he can no longer look without touching.

Then, it's up to him. Sometimes, Tim takes his cock and rubs the head against me, without even entering me just yet. It's not about getting inside but about watching the collision of our bodies, watching the collusion, watching hard meet soft, covering himself with my dew as he parses every second out into a slow-motion image he'll replay in his mind. It's like an introduction, a getting-to-know-you greeting for someone you've seen around for years but want to reacquaint yourself with. I, in turn, watch him, watch his eyes riveted to that spot where his cockhead is starting to make me truly ache, the dull throb moving from the entrance to my hole all the way inside, tunneling through me until I feel hollow. The longer he does it, the longer the ache lasts; I've often woken up the next day with a pang so strong I clutch him, then shove my fingers inside myself to try to quell it. Looking at his face, I'm no longer blushing, but biting my lower lip, swirling my tongue over the soft, plump pinkness as my teeth dig into the paler flesh beneath my lip. Watching him watching me, watching us, is the hottest live-action porn I'll ever see.

So his request to see what I do when I'm alone shakes me up. That is not what I'd consider pretty or anything close to foreplay material. Unlike our pre-sex ritual, it's not leading up to anything; my masturbation is the main event, no need to lure anyone in with a preview. I can be lying in bed reading, lounging there in silk pajamas one moment—and the next, naked, on all fours, long hair tossed to the side while I ride my plug-in vibe hard, bucking up and down against it. When I get myself off, it's not a Georgia O'Keefe painting come to life. It's not a slow-build, soft-focus, petal-parting anything. Granted, we don't always exist in the rose-colored gloss of gentle grinding, Tim and I. When he's had his fill of watching, of filling me with a burn so hot I've been known to draw blood from sinking my top teeth into my lower lip, he slams his cock into me so swiftly and strongly I often come right then and there. By that time, I don't care what he sees, what he cracks open inside my skull as he screws me like there's no tomorrow. That phrase sounds trite only if you've never done it so hard you don't care if it's your last breath, so hard that nothing else exists. I don't care if he sees me sniveling, crying out, contorted, aching for him while he's fucking me, because I know, even if I'm too overwhelmed to do anything but shut my eyes, what he's feeling. It's the two of us against the world, and there's no question who's going to win.

Still, I'm nervous that he won't like what he sees. That I won't like what he sees, that this will shatter some fifth wall that makes our relationship work, removing all mystery. Because the truth is, my masturbation sessions are, in their own way, even fiercer than that, fiercer than when he skips the preliminaries and slams me up against today's chosen piece of furniture—the bed, the couch, a chair, the sink—and fucks me with his fingers in my mouth, his cock so deep inside me it feels like a part of my body. When I'm alone, all bets are off. I'm so far from pornographic I'm into grotesque. At least, to my mind. I don't think about what I look like when it's just me and one of my trusty vibrators, me letting out all the things I can't find release for in everyday life. In fact, I try not to think too much at all—it kills the mood. I just go with what I feel.

But this is Tim, my Tim, after all. He's asking, with a look so open on his face I can't deny him. I know he loves every inch of my body, so even though I'm still unsure, I settle him at the far end of our bed, with me on the other, and set forth. "Okay, but I've warned you. Sit right there and don't come any closer. I do it like this," I say, and then turn on the vibrator. At first, I have to pretend to myself he's not there. He may be my husband but he is still a spectator, someone invading my private, very personal ritual, even though I've invited him. He knows I masturbate, but knowing and seeing are two different things. "Unh," I say out loud as the power of the toy propels me somewhere else, somewhere far from my marital bed.

I will my mind to forget Tim, to forget everything as I lift one leg up onto the wall, grateful for all the yoga I've taken that makes me limber enough to reach the positions that get me off best. With one foot flattened against the wall, I stretch the other one out to my side as the round, white head of the electric miracle glides against my clit, seeking the right spot to call home. With my left hand, I reach up for the headboard, needing the strain of muscle in my arms and legs to loop back through my body to my clit. Without that, the vibrations are meaningless. Strong, sure, but just not enough. I let out a shuddery breath that brings tears to my eyes as the curved white head sinks deeper into me, nudging against the top of my pussy while still giving ample sensation to my clit. Soon it will be time to stuff something inside me, too. Sometimes it's my fingers, sometimes a toy, sometimes whatever's handy. I once used a fat magic marker, circling it and feeling the tip pressing against my G-spot. I'll try anything when I'm alone, but with Tim as my VIP audience member, suddenly I'm flustered.

It doesn't matter that he will be happy with whatever I show him, that in fact, he doesn't want a "show" but reality. That ups the ante all the more, because no matter how much I pretend, I'm not alone. There he is, and I hope that what he sees won't change what he thinks of me. But then my fantasy life takes over, the one where it's not just Tim but Liza, too. A smile breaks out across my face as I spread my legs even wider, practically shoving the buzzing toy into my clit, slamming it hard as I contort and become one with my vibrator and thoughts of a threesome with my husband and gorgeous best friend. It's never going to happen, but that hasn't stopped me from wanking my way to countless orgasms thinking about it. I wet my fingers with my mouth and shove them deep inside me while I rock, knowing I'm blocking his view for a minute, but not caring. Then that becomes too much, and I lean back, part my legs, and do some snooping of my own. I sneak a peek through my slitted eyes at Tim; he's got his hand on his cock, his eyes fixed on my cunt, and he looks like he's halfway to orgasm himself.

Rather than making me nervous, this spurs me on. He likes what he sees; maybe I don't look so weird, after all. I turn the vibrator down to a lower level and move more slowly, letting my body do more of the work. I let the few tears that have been hovering at my eyelids drop onto my cheeks. I flip over onto my stomach so my ass—the one Tim's always wanting to grab, slap, and bite, the one I always thought was too big and too round before we met—is right in his face. For a few seconds, I remove the vibrator and spread my lips for him, hoping he's watching. I've never done that before when it wasn't an invitation to come inside, no RSVP required. Now it's more of a "look what I've got, don't you wish you could touch it?" parting of my pussy lips, and the power of holding, and withholding, races through me. I turn the vibrator back on and settle down onto it, letting it rest against the bed as I straddle it. I feel even more exposed like this, but it reminds me of my favorite fantasy, the one where I'm face down, my head buried in Liza's pussy, while Tim plows me from behind. The harder he fucks me, the deeper my tongue slams into her, so it's almost like he's fucking her. I like the idea of being the middleman, or middlewoman, as the case may be, my body just a conduit for their pleasure, even as the mere thought of it sends juices leaking down my inner thighs.

I lean my head against a pillow, burying my face in its soft, clean whiteness. I'm probably blushing because even though Tim's behind me, it feels like he can see inside me, too, as if baring myself like this means giving him free reign over my thoughts.

What would he make of them? Would my most twisted fantasies turn him on or send him away? I realize as I turn the vibrator back to high, its screeching permeating the room, drowning out my panting as I then plunge my fingers inside my pussy, that it doesn't matter. All Tim can see is my spread legs, my ass, my cunt, my fingers, my toy. He sees only what I allow him to, nothing more. I start to hear his grunts over the noise of the vibe and when I look over, his hand's moving at lightning speed. I turn over once again onto my back and watch him master his own unguarded bliss. At the money shot, his eyes are closed and he's as gone as I've wanted to be this whole time. I'd thought I was there, but until I see him let go 100 percent, I can't truly relax. Once he's done, it's like I have permission. I've been putting on a show, however subtle, instead of giving him what he wanted, the antithesis of a performance. I'm his wife, and yet it feels like until today we've hardly known each other.

Armed with the blessing of his orgasm, I let go once and for all. I growl, I moan, I thrash. I beat the toy against my cunt so hard that it hurts, but I like it and want more. I think about me and Tim and Liza, about strangers invading our bed, about two cocks in my mouth at once. I twist into a ball, toss aside the toy, and press my palm against my hot flesh. I pinch and tug and pull on my clit until the most strangled scream erupts from my throat. I shove as many fingers as I can get into my pussy and squeeze them tight. My climax is the kind that rushes up to me and then takes its time, hopping forward, sliding back, dancing some mixed-up fusion mambosalsabreakdancebeat until I'm slain, caught, trapped between its jerky hands and quick hips, its tornado-like swirl capturing me. That's how it feels when I come like this, not like a speeding bullet but a fireball bursting into flame, the embers echoing through my limbs until I'm burned to a crisp.

When I'm done, I summon just enough energy to turn off the toy. I stay huddled in my personal shell, wondering if I'm now too naked, too exposed, if both of us have ventured to the point of no return. Tim takes the purple blanket I knitted for us after our honeymoon, the one with the holes and splatters, and covers me with it, kisses me on my forehead, and whispers in my ear, "That was beautiful. You're beautiful. Just like this." Then he leaves me to myself, my dreams, my questions, my pounding heart that's slowly coming down from the ledge. I bring my fingers between my legs, press them against my skin, and wait to drift off.

When I wake up in the middle of the night, he's next to me, naked, sprawled every which way. I peek at him in repose, stare my fill, before tossing off the blanket myself. I want to be more naked for him from now on, want to take some of the magic of this night and hold onto it, use it to see each other as only we can. He may not know it yet, but he's unleashed a monster. This was just the beginning.

ABOUT THE AUTHORS

L. ELISE BLAND never travels without her diary. Dominatrix, stripper, naked actress—she's done it all and has lived to write about it in both fact and fiction. Her most recent publications include *Secret Slaves: Erotic Stories of Bondage* (Alyson), *Naughty Spanking Stories from A to Z 2* (Pretty Things Press), *Best American Erotica 2006* (Fireside/Touchstone), and *First-Timers: True Stories of Lesbian Awakening* (Alyson). Learn more about her writings at www.lelisebland.com.

LEE CAIRNEY lives in East Anglia, England. She's interested in writing about sex and the imaginative loophole sex creates out of the boring contract of everyday life. She's also interested in sex. "Cruising" is her first foray into the dirty and demanding twilight world, or so she likes to imagine it, of women's erotica.

MATT CONKLIN is a confirmed sadist with a weakness for pretty girls. He's been in the scene for over a decade but is always in search of the perfect sub. His erotica has also been published in *He's on Top*.

PORTIA DA COSTA has been writing erotic bestsellers, both raw and romantic, for more years than she cares to remember. Author of over twenty novels and almost a hundred short stories, she's noted for tales of kinky sexual fun told with a warm, emotional heart. Her recent titles include *Entertaining Mr. Stone, Gothic Blue, Suite Seventeen,* and a paranormal novella, *Buddies Don't Bite*.

ANDREA DALE's stories have appeared in *Got a Minute?, C Is for Coeds,* and *Ultimate Lesbian Erotica 2007,* and on Fishnetmag.com. With co-authors, she has sold novels to Cheek Books (*A Little Night Music*, Sarah Dale) and Black Lace Books (*Cat Scratch Fever,* Sophie Mouette). She lives in Southern California within scent of the ocean and can sometimes be persuaded to bake at Christmas. Her website is at www.cyvarwydd.com.

DANTE DAVIDSON is a tenured professor in Santa Barbara, California. His short stories have appeared in *Bondage* (Masquerade), *Naughty Stories from A to Z* (PTP), *Best Bondage Erotica* (Cleis), *Merry XXXmas* (Cleis), and *Sweet Life* (Cleis). With Alison Tyler, he is the co-author of the best-selling collection of short fiction *Bondage on a Budget* (PTP) and *Secrets for Great Sex After Fifty* (which he wrote at age 28).

For more than 20 years, **ERICA DEQUAYA** has padded her bank account as a journalist, copywriter, and scriptwriter (with two produced plays under her belt). During the past several years, she's turned to writing erotica romances. Her novels include the critically acclaimed *Backstage Affair* and *Mixed Media,* which was winner of the Road to Romance "Recommended Read" award. She's also dabbled in the sensual side of hockey players and their lady lovers with novels *Power Play* and *In the Crease* and short story "Penalty Kill." Erica lives in Texas with her husband/soul mate of more than two decades, her son, and two neurotic dogs. Visit myspace.com/ericadequaya for more information.

SHANNA GERMAIN is a poet by nature, a short story writer by the skin of her teeth, and a novelist in training. You can read her work in a variety of places, including *Absinthe Literary Review*, *Best American Erotica 2007*, *Bondage Erotica 2*, *Best Gay Romance 2008*, *Caught Looking*, *Got a Minute?*, and *Naughty or Nice*.

MICHELLE HOUSTON has been writing erotica since 1995 and has had stories published in many anthologies, including *D Is for Dress-Up*, *Naughty Stories from A to Z vol. 4*, *Threeway*, *Naughty Spanking Stories from A to Z vol. 2*, *The Merry XXXmas Book of Erotica*, *C Is for Coeds*, and *Slave to Love*. In addition to her print publications, she also has several of her own e-books and stories in a couple of other e-books. You can find out more about her and her writings on her personal website, The Erotic Pen: http://www.eroticpen.net.

DEBRA HYDE's erotic fiction appears in many Cleis Press anthologies, such as *She's on Top*, *He's on Top*, *Caught Looking*, and *The Happy Birthday Book of Erotica*. Her first erotic novel, *Inequities*, is available in the British Commonwealth, but if that's too far-flung for you, you can visit her at her long-running weblog, Pursed Lips, or listen to her via her occasional podcast, Pursed Lips, Speaking. Debra's been known to have hotel sex with the curtains open, just in case someone's looking.

STAN KENT is a chameleon-hair-colored, former-nightclub-owning, rocket-scientist author of erotic novels. A dedicated voyeur and lover of shoes, boots, and the women wearing them, Stan has penned nine original, unique, and very naughty works, including the *Shoe Leather* series. His short stories have been featured in *Caught Looking, Ultimate Undies, Sexiest Soles,* and *Naughty Spanking Stories from A to Z 2*. Stan has hosted an erotic talk-show night at Hustler Hollywood, where the *Los Angeles Times* described his monthly performances as "combination moderator and lion tamer." To see samples of his works and his latest hair colors, visit Stan at www.StanKent.com or email him at stan@stankent.com.

CHERI MAGID writes a popular erotic blog and a column under various and sundry pseudonyms. She is also a playwright whose work has been seen in New York, California, Ohio, Iowa, and Michigan. *Lydia, or The Girl at the Wheel,* Cheri's radio play about the earliest days of burlesque, aired on National Public Radio in 2001. She is currently writing a screenplay, *The Story of D,* about the real story behind the writing of *The Story of O,* for Dan Wigutow Productions.

GWEN MASTERS is a writer, publisher, songwriter, editor, and guitar slinger's muse. She is the author of a handful of novels and too many short stories to count, most of which have appeared in print sometime over the last ten years. To learn more about Gwen and her naughty tales, visit her website at www.gwenmasters.net.

L.A. MISTRAL's novels *Seminary of the Seven Veils* and *The Latin Tutor* can be seen in the "sizzling" section of Renaissance e-books. He also publishes reviews, essays, and poetry. His most

ABOUT THE AUTHORS

recent short stories appear in print in *B Is for Bondage* and *Got a Minute?*, both edited by Alison Tyler.

RADCLYFFE is the author of over twenty-five lesbian novels and anthologies, including the 2005 Lambda Literary Award winners *Erotic Interludes 2: Stolen Moments*, edited with Stacia Seaman, and the romance, *Distant Shores, Silent Thunder*. She has selections in many anthologies, including *Best Lesbian Erotica 2006* and *2007*, *Caught Looking: Erotic Tales of Voyeurs and Exhibitionists*, *First-Timers*, *Ultimate Undies: Erotic Stories About Lingerie and Underwear*, and *Naughty Spanking Stories from A to Z 2*. She is also the president of Bold Strokes Books, a lesbian publishing company.

TERESA NOELLE ROBERTS's erotica has appeared or is forthcoming in *He's on Top*, *She's on Top*, *B Is for Bondage*, *E Is for Exotic*, *F Is for Fetish*, *H Is for Hardcore*, *Chocolate Flava 2*, *Best Women's Erotica 2004*, *2005*, and *2007*, and many other publications. She is also half of the erotica-writing team called Sophie Mouette, author of *Cat Scratch Fever* (Black Lace Books 2006).

THOMAS S. ROCHE is an author of erotica, horror, crime fiction, and fantasy, as well as nonfiction on related topics. More than 400 of his short stories have been published in a wide variety of magazines, including the *Best American Erotica* series and the *Best New Erotica* series. Roche also works in the field of sex education for the nonprofit San Francisco Sex Information (www.sfsi.org) and runs the Barbary Coast edition of the notorious Dr. Sketchy's Anti-Art School burlesque figure-drawing salon. He is the managing editor of Eros Zine (www.eros-zine.com) and can also be found online at Skid Roche (www.skidroche.com).

SASKIA WALKER's erotic fiction appears in over forty anthologies, including *Caught Looking, She's on Top, Slave to Love, Secrets vol. 15, The Mammoth Book of Best New Erotica vol. 5, Stirring Up a Storm,* and *Kink.* She is the author of several novellas as well as the erotic novels *Along for the Ride, Double Dare,* and *Reckless.* Please visit www.saskiawalker.co.uk for more information.

KRISTINA WRIGHT's erotic fiction has appeared in over forty anthologies, including four editions of the Lambda Literary Award–winning series *Best Lesbian Erotica,* two editions of *Best Women's Erotica,* and two volumes of the *Mammoth Book of Best New Erotica.* Her work has also been featured in the nonfiction guide *The Many Joys of Sex Toys* and in such e-zines as *Clean Sheets, Scarlet Letters,* and *Good Vibes Magazine.* Kristina holds a BA in English and an MA in Humanities. For more information, visit her website www.kristinawright.com.

ABOUT THE EDITORS

RACHEL KRAMER BUSSEL is a prolific erotica writer, editor, journalist, and blogger. She serves as senior editor at *Penthouse Variations*, hosts the In the Flesh Erotic Reading Series, and wrote the popular Lusty Lady column for *The Village Voice*. Her books include *Naughty Spanking Stories from A to Z 1* and *2*, *First-Timers*, *Up All Night*, *Glamour-Girls: Femme/Femme Erotica*, *Ultimate Undies*, *Sexiest Soles*, *Secret Slaves: Erotic Stories of Bondage*, *Sex and Candy: Sugar Erotica*, *Caught Looking: Erotic Tales of Voyeurs and Exhibitionism*, *Crossdressing*, *Best Sex Writing 2008*, and the kinky companion volumes *He's on Top: Erotic Stories of Male Dominance and Female Submission* and *She's on Top: Erotic Stories of Female Dominance and Male Dominance*. Her twin odes to bottoming, *Yes, Sir: Erotic Stories of Female Submission and Male Dominance* and *Yes, Ma'am: Erotic Stories of Male Submission and Female Dominance*, will be published by Cleis Press in February 2008, and her first novel, *Everything But...*, will be published by Bantam in summer 2008.

Her writing has been published in over 100 anthologies, including *Best American Erotica 2004* and *2006*, as well as *AVN, Bust,* Cleansheets.com, *Cosmo UK, Diva, Girlfriends,* Huffington Post, Mediabistro.com, *New York Post,* Oxygen.com, *Penthouse, Playgirl, Punk Planet, San Francisco Chronicle, Time Out New York,* and *Zink.* In her spare time, she hunts down the country's best cupcakes and blogs about them at cupcakestakethecake.blogspot.com. Visit her at www.rachelkramerbussel.com.

Called a "literary siren" by Good Vibrations, **ALISON TYLER** is naughty and she knows it. She is author of a collection of short erotic fiction, *Exposed* (Cleis Press), and more than twenty explicit novels, including *Rumors, Tiffany Twisted,* and *With or Without You* (all published by Cheek), and the winner of "best kinky sex scene" as awarded by *Scarlet Magazine.* Her novels and short stories have been translated into Japanese, Dutch, German, Italian, Norwegian, Greek, and Spanish.

According to Clean Sheets, "Alison Tyler has introduced readers to some of the hottest contemporary erotica around." And she's done so through the editing of more than thirty-five sexy anthologies, including the erotic alphabet series (*A Is for Amour, B Is for Bondage, C Is for Coeds, D Is for Dress-Up...*), all published by Cleis Press, as well as the *Naughty Stories from A to Z* series, the *Down & Dirty* series, *Naked Erotica,* and *Juicy Erotica* (all from Pretty Things Press). Please drop by www.prettythingspress.com.

Ms. Tyler is loyal to coffee (black), lipstick (red), and tequila (straight). She has tattoos but no piercings, a wicked tongue but a quick smile, and bittersweet memories but no regrets. She believes it won't rain if she doesn't bring an umbrella, prefers hot and dry to cold and wet, and loves to spout her favorite motto: "You can sleep when you're dead." She chooses Led Zeppelin

ABOUT THE EDITOR

over the Beatles, the Cure over NIN, and the Stones over everyone—yet although she appreciates good rock, she has a pitiful weakness for eighties hair bands. In all things important, she remains faithful to her partner of more than a decade, but she still can't settle on one perfume.

Visit www.alisontyler.com for more luscious revelations or myspace.com/alisontyler if you'd like to be her friend.